Initial
SHOCK

Mary Flynn

DEDICATION

*To The Lord himself,
who must have decided early on
to give me something
I might end up being any good at.*

"No man chooses evil because it is evil;
he mistakes it for happiness."

— *Mary Shelley*

OTHER BOOKS BY MARY FLYNN

— Fiction —

Margaret Ferry

The Flower Cottage

No Small Wonder

Wishbones and Other Short Stories

— Poetry —

As One Delighted

— Non-fiction —

Disney's "Secret Sauce"

The Little-Known Factor BEHIND...

The Business World's MOST LEGENDARY LEADERSHIP

— Children's —

Reggie & Rocky

The Ring-tailed Raccoons

Reggie & Rocky

The Naughty Raccoons

— Middle Grade —

Mrs. Peppel's Pillows

ACKNOWLEDGEMENT

It is impossible to jot down a single acknowledgement without first tipping my hat to Agatha Christie and Sir Arthur Conan Doyle who captured my imagination nearly from the moment I started reading full-length books. It always suited me that there was no extravagant throat-slitting—just a cozy little dead body here and there combined with clever deception and brilliant sleuthing. I humbly aspire to, somehow, even come close. As always, I want to thank my editor/proofreader, the wonderful Ann Frailey, along with my dear friends and trusted beta readers Jean Apuzzo and Fred Gray. And, of course, my fabulous Graphic Arts Designer, Mike Butler at Michael by Design, whose cover art and layout are always so beautifully done. I am forever grateful, as well, to the dedicated and determined Sisters of St. Joseph, who drilled into every one of the thirty-nine children in their Brooklyn classrooms that there was nearly nothing else at that point in our young lives as important as literacy. And, finally, I thank my readers, without whom … well … what's the point?

CHAPTER ONE

—————«*Westport, Connecticut — 1940*

THE CAR SWERVED, and Claire opened her eyes to the darkness of the unfamiliar Connecticut countryside.

"Sorry. Raccoon," the driver said in the same gravelly voice he had apologized for earlier. "Laryngitis." He tugged at his chauffeur's cap, the collar of his black coat pulled up around his neck, even though the car had warmed considerably since they'd left the train station. Nice of her uncle to have sent a private car.

The clock on the dashboard said 6:10. She glanced out at the pitch-dark woods flanking the narrow, winding incline, while Glenn Miller's "Tuxedo Junction" played on the radio. She undid the top button of her wool coat, then loosened her scarf, grateful that she had done one final weather-check before leaving Chicago. Her trench coat would never have done well against this early October New England cold snap.

Her uncle had told her it shouldn't be more than a twenty-five-minute ride. She retrieved the hair brush from her train case, certain that fatigue had already added a decade to her twenty-nine years. She wasn't sure which had been more exhausting, the long, tiring journey by train from Chicago or her nervousness about seeing her uncle, more like a first meeting really—it had been years.

His original offer might have been the wisest choice, after all—sending his car to meet her at Grand Central Station. But she wouldn't hear of it. The situation was awkward enough without imposing any more than was necessary. He would simply have a car waiting once she arrived from the city to take her to the estate.

She removed the hatpin from the back of her cloche, placed the hat on the seat beside her, then worked her hair brush through a tangle of soft waves, wondering if she should have stayed overnight in Manhattan and arrived at her uncle's, rested, a day later. Instead, she had persisted in making it in one tiring stretch.

"Just a bit longer," the driver said in a throaty whisper, as if sensing Claire's weary restlessness.

With only the faint illumination of the lighted dashboard, Claire could no longer make out very much about him beneath the line of his cap, but judging by the ease of his movements on the dark, winding hills, he was experienced and reliable behind the wheel, qualifications that The Village Limousine Company no doubt valued highly in drivers of estates' clientele. Still, there was something about him that added ever so slightly to her anxiety.

Claire closed her eyes and drew a deep breath, tired from hours of sitting, hours spent re-creating in her mind the various composites of her uncle, shaped over the years from the praiseful reminiscences of his sister, Evelyn Farrow.

Aunt Evelyn had adored her slightly reclusive, wealthy younger brother. She had always said that if she ever found a single thing in Paul Farrow that needed forgiving, she would forgive it at once. Would Claire be able to overlook the fact that Paul Farrow missed the funeral of this handsome, witty woman, so wise and full of spirit, who had been more a mother than an aunt to Claire? It had not been easy for Claire to forgive her uncle for missing Evelyn's funeral. But she did forgive him. Evelyn would have. And, after all, it was reasonable that a bad case of influenza could prevent his making the trip for the funeral Mass.

"I would give anything to come," he had said to Claire on the day he was to have arrived in Chicago, his voice deep and somber. Claire was angry at first, though she didn't express it, then relieved not to have added to an unbearably difficult time the complication of standing on ceremony with an uncle who was little more than a beloved character in someone else's memory. In her entire life, Claire had perhaps a half dozen telephone conversations with him, each a brief and polite exchange. But she must not overlook the fact that he had taken full responsibility in the past few years for the care of his long-time friend and fellow architect who had suffered a severe, debilitating stroke.

She yawned and laid her head back, envisioning the hot shower and soft bed that would come at the end of all the polite conversation she really wasn't up to. She wouldn't be here at all if it weren't for the "loose ends," as her aunt's attorneys in New York had called them, vestiges of Evelyn's affairs that required Claire's signature on a document here, an affidavit there. And while in New York, why not satisfy this irrepressible need to meet the only relative she had left in the world?

Frank Sinatra sang "Polka Dots and Moonbeams" on the car radio just before the bleak news—Mussolini's army on the move after invading Albania, Hitler's defeat of France. Maybe now with Churchill as England's new Prime Minister, things would change. She prayed that the United States would not enter the war.

Another swerve. More raccoons, she guessed. This time, the car swung out with a sweeping arc across the roadway, its lights slashing wildly in the wooded darkness. "Whoa! Hey! Driver!" She yelled, grabbing at anything to hold onto as she pitched from one side of the car to the other. "Driver!" She yelled again, as something at the road's edge caught the headlight's beam and shimmered momentarily. The car had gained momentum. In the darkness, she could make out the driver throwing the wheel left, then right as, more than once, Claire nearly hit her head against the window.

In seconds, they were beyond the road's graveled shoulder and jouncing down a steep, wooded slope, tearing noisily through thick brush like a lumbering animal. Claire's mind raced with the terrifying possibilities—a fiery crash, a fatal accident. The interior lights went out, and she felt a rush of frigid air. "Hey! Driver!" she yelled. "What's happening?" In the ragged blips of light, she could see that he was gone. The rough descent ended with a whooshing sound. Loud static replaced the music, then silence. Amid her stream of gasps, she felt a cushioning sensation. "Oh, God! Water! Driver, help!" Nothing. She could tell that the driver's door was wide open. He must have been thrown out. "Dear Lord!"

As the car tipped downward, Claire pushed at her door but couldn't open it. She grabbed hold of the crank handle to roll down the window, but it was impossible to turn; the window wouldn't budge. She could hear the water rushing in and knew she had to get out through the driver's door before the suction pulled her down with the car. With the vehicle gulping icy water, she managed to pull herself up and over the front seat. If she didn't drown, she would certainly freeze to death.

The car tipped farther forward and to the left as if about to roll over. Claire slammed into some hard surface, disoriented and unsure whether it was a door or the roof. The car lunged, and she fell against the steering wheel. The water was over the dashboard now. She called out, her worst fear that there was no one to help, no one who would even be aware of what was going on. Frantic, she felt around in the darkness for the driver, certain now that he must have fallen out the front door. "Lord!"

The car was nearly vertical, on its way down, the rising water past her shoulders. She held onto the steering wheel, knowing the open door was right there, and lunged toward the opening as the water sucked at her ankles, pulling her back. She tore at the buttons of her heavy coat and let it fall away. Free of the extra weight, she took a deep breath and went under, swimming and kicking with all her might, losing one of her shoes. The car went down quickly, creating a drag on her body. She pushed to reach the surface of the water.

Seconds later, her heart hammering away, she emerged, gasping, then thrashed toward the dark shape of land as a new fear gripped her—might she be greeted by some slithery creature inhabiting the water's edge? She realized she had only two options, and she had just escaped one of them. Her only other fear was that the driver did not have the same good fortune.

She kept on until the water became shallow enough for her to feel its stony bottom underfoot, then staggered through a narrow, fencelike stand of low grass, collapsing face down on a sloping bank redolent of pine and mossy dampness. She lay there unable to move, unable to feel the cold, every part of her body throbbing. If she didn't get help soon, she would die of hypothermia.

Barely conscious, she heard a noise, the soft crackling of footsteps in the nearby brush. Someone approaching. Thank God. A faint sweep of light came from what must have been a hilltop, accompanied by the distant sound of excited voices.

"Here," she strained to call out. "Here." Her voice had no strength left. Lightheaded and fearful of passing out, she heard someone walk around her. Now on the brink of unconsciousness, she could feel nothing except a queer tightening sensation on her ankles. Someone was pulling her. Her feet tingled with icy cold. No! No! She was being pulled back into the water.

There was another sweep of light, this one closer, and voices growing louder, nearer, before Claire stopped hearing them altogether.

Chapter Two

"Claire?"

It drifted through the misty silence of her mind. A voice. A word. A whispered question in the gray void.

"Claire Fournaris?"

She forced her eyes open to see a foggy slit of light that held two blurry faces, one of them a man's round face. He was speaking.

"I'm Doctor Gomshay, Claire. Can you hear me? You're doing fine. You're going to be all right. You're safe now."

Claire could barely blink him into focus, a great, pleasant face with a rubbery pinkness. He had thick gray hair and mustache, with eyebrows the texture of steel wool.

She slowly moved her eyes to the other face, also a man's, younger, darker, somber by contrast.

"Miss Fournaris? I'm Lieutenant Frank Desiata of the Village Police. You're in the hospital not far from your uncle's estate. You've been here since last evening. It's now seven o'clock Tuesday evening. May I please ask you a few questions? Just a few, I promise."

Claire stirred uneasily with the first vague recollection of her ordeal and groaned from the soreness of her body. There was a drip line attached to her arm.

"You're going to be a bit stiff for a time," Gomshay said. "But otherwise, you're just fine. You've also had some medication that may make you feel a little fuzzy. That's okay too. You've been through a lot. Just relax and take things slowly. We're here to help."

Claire turned her head slowly to survey the room, expecting the harsh white and metal surroundings of another hospital where, years before, her mother had taken four months to succumb to the tuberculosis that had resisted every treatment. Instead, her fragile consciousness took in the soft illumination of lamplight on mauve walls, where there were pictures, and a vase of flowers set on a table across the room.

A man in a dark suit sat cross-legged in a chair near the window. Dr. Gomshay introduced him as David Preisler, her uncle's assistant. Claire knew the name from Evelyn. He came forward and stood at the foot of the bed. "I'm glad to see you're finally awake." He was a nice-looking man about in his thirties, she guessed, dark hair, tall. He smiled.

"David has been here most of the time since you were brought in," said Gomshay. "He and Louis Joel, your uncle's chauffeur, are the ones who found you."

David Preisler smiled. "Of course, we had no idea who was in the car up ahead that had suddenly gone off the road and into the woods."

Gomshay patted Claire's hand. "A great stroke of luck, I'd say."

She remembered distant voices. "Thank you." The words cracked in her dry throat.

Dr. Gomshay poured a small cup of water and lifted Claire's head to help her sip, as Lieutenant Desiata pulled a chair to the side of the bed and sat.

"Miss Fournaris, I know you're weak. Forgive me, but I must ask a few questions." Desiata leafed through the pages of his small spiral pad and reached into his inside suit pocket for a pen. "Can you tell me, as best you can, what happened last night? How the accident occurred, and what followed?"

Slowly, Claire began telling of the otherwise uneventful car ride and of the driver losing control on the winding road. She jerked upright. "The driver!" She looked with urgency from face to face, her stomach tightening. "Is he all right? I … I couldn't find him." She collapsed in pain against the pillow. "He was thrown from the car."

"We don't know yet," said the lieutenant. "We're still searching. We were hoping you'd be able to tell us something that might help."

Claire pressed her eyes shut at the prospect of the man's death, a man who, despite his best efforts to save their lives, had likely lost his own. "It was dark. I was so scared."

"Was there anyone else in the car?"

"No."

Gomshay gave her a little more water.

She sipped sparingly and went on. "When the car finally stopped, I didn't realize at first that we were … that we were in the water. I kept calling for the driver. I thought he might be slumped over. I yelled for help. I reached all around in the front seat as I … as I tried to get out. The water was coming in so fast, but there was no sign of him."

"Could he have been on the floor?" Desiata asked.

"No. I would have touched him in some way. The driver door was open. That's why … that's why I was sure he'd been thrown out." She paused to catch her breath.

"Take your time," Desiata said.

"I was terrified. The front of the car was heading down. I had a feeling the water might be very deep."

"Yes, very," Desiata said.

"Do you think there's any possibility that he might be alive? That he … that he might have made it to shore, same as I did?"

"After being on the force for nineteen years, Miss Fournaris, I've come to believe there is very little in this world that *isn't* possible. He could have surfaced on another part of the shore and may be wandering in shock somewhere. He could also have been rescued by someone, same as you."

Her eyes widened. "It was so cold. How long could he survive without help?"

Desiata looked up at Gomshay, then back at Claire. "Please don't upset yourself. We're looking at this from every angle. So, let's wait and see. I'll be sure to keep you posted."

When he was gone, Claire felt exhausted. Dr. Gomshay departed with a few pleasant words and a promise to check on her later. "For now, let's just get all the rest we can."

"Thank you, Doctor. I … I appreciate all that you're doing for me."

With the others gone, David Preisler came around to the side of the bed, smiling. "The peonies are from your uncle." He gestured to the vase of flowers. "He was here earlier, and last night after they brought you in."

"Please thank him for me." She looked at Preisler. "How did anyone know who I am? My identification … everything was in the car."

"Your uncle identified you."

"As if I were a corpse."

"It does sound that way, doesn't it? At any rate, he had a picture of you. It's the only way we could be certain who you were. When Louis and I found you, we had an inkling you might be Paul's niece. Strangers rarely use that road. It's more or less a private route, being somewhat out of the way as it is. Even the Village Taxi Company doesn't take passengers up without authorization from a particular estate. We knew you were due to arrive at any time and that your uncle was to have the taxi meet your train."

"I'm … grateful to you both."

He took a pack of Camels from his suit pocket. "You mind?"

She shook her head.

"Actually," he said, tossing the match into a glass ashtray, "your uncle had originally planned to pick you up, but he had to change his plans because of an important phone call that ended up on his schedule, one that he couldn't change. The only reason he booked the taxi was because Louis and I were not available. Good thing we happened to be heading back to the estate precisely when we did.

"How did you even find me?"

"This is where the lucky part comes in." He pulled his chair a little closer to the bed. "We were driving up that road toward the house. There was a car a good distance in front of us. The car began to swerve, and we saw the lights flashing through the woods to the left ahead of us. We realized it had to be that car. We pulled over, got the flashlights out of the trunk, and made our way down. When we didn't see anything, we realized the car was already in the water. We didn't know it was a taxi at that point, but we knew it was sinking fast. Thank God we found you."

"No sign of the driver?"

"Nothing. Later on, of course, Village Taxi confirmed that a car had been dispatched to meet a Miss Fournaris at the train station and take her to the Farrow estate. Louis called the house; you hadn't arrived. It all fit."

She turned away. "That poor driver."

"He might be all right. We don't know." Preisler looked at his watch and got to his feet, tamping his cigarette in the ashtray. "I'd better leave you to rest." He tossed his coat over his arm. "Gomshay will be furious if he finds out I'm still here. Everything will be all right." He smiled. "Who knows—the driver might be somewhere recovering just as you are." Then, leaving only a small corner lamp, he turned off the lights and said he'd see her in the morning.

As he opened the door to leave, Claire called out, "Wait! My luggage. All my things."

"Lost, I'm sorry to say. For the time being, anyway."

She struggled to raise herself on one elbow, then fell back in pain.

David rushed to the side of the bed. "Hey, take it easy now. You heard the doctor."

"But what'll I do about clothes, money? My driver's license, my keys?"

"Don't worry about any of that now," he said. "Some things may be retrieved. We'll just have to see; the lake is pretty deep, so it may take a while." He tucked in the end of her bed sheet. "Tell you what—tomorrow, we'll make a list, and I'll personally pick up everything that's on it."

"I can't let you do that." Her voice cracked. "I don't even know you. I don't know anyone here. Not even my uncle."

"I forget who said, 'You're only a stranger once,' but it's not a bad take on life. By tomorrow, we'll be good friends."

He had a kind enough look about him—warm eyes, a smile that seemed sincere. "Thank you again," she said, barely able to get the words out, as the medicine took hold. "Thanks to all … of you."

"Till tomorrow." He winked and was gone.

The room fell peacefully silent. Claire lay still, exhausted, and wary now of any move that would bring on pain. Was there something else to tell the police officer? Something … important? She drifted into the enveloping calm, wishing only to go back into that gray void and come out the other side, in her own bed, with nothing more troubling than the fading recollection of a bad dream. She might even find that all the grief of the last few weeks was only part of this same nightmare, and that Aunt Evelyn wasn't dead, after all. But even in her muddled, wishful mind, she was gripped by some odd sense that she was not at all out of danger.

Chapter Three

Claire drifted deeper into the murky silence. Deeper, the water within a foot of the roof. She went under, trying to wriggle through the open doorway, kicking to free herself. The car was going down quickly now. She struggled toward the surface, unable to hold her breath any longer, her heavy, water-soaked coat weighing her down. She needed to reach the air. She needed to breathe. The coat wouldn't come off. She pulled at the sleeves. She needed air. She pulled and kicked. There was no air! No air!

"What's happening here?" Dr. Gomshay rushed toward the bed where two nurses struggled to subdue Claire's flailing arms.

"We heard a commotion, Doctor," one of the nurses said, "and when we got here, she was hanging out of the bed, headfirst, gasping and sobbing. Her pillows were on the floor, and her bed covers were all pulled apart. She had even knocked her water pitcher off the table."

"A nightmare," said the other nurse.

Gomshay stepped closer. "No point being alarmed. I'm sure she'll have more, after what she's been through. Let's get her straightened around and comfortable. And keep a close watch on her."

"Sedate?"

"By all means." Gomshay looked at Claire dolefully as the nurses settled her back on the bed. "Miss Fournaris, you're going to be fine. Please know that. These dreams will fade away."

Claire looked up, dazed, and without responding, finally closed her eyes.

After jotting some notes on Claire's chart, Gomshay followed the nurses out of the room. A few minutes later, one of the nurses returned with a sedative. Almost as soon as Claire felt the jarring pinch of the needle, the gray void began to overtake her. She heard the nurse go out. Then, the door opened again, and with a dreamy gaze, she caught a blurred, dark figure moving out of the room and into the corridor. At the same time, the closet door a few feet away slowly closed. That figure! Coat collar pulled up! Then, only the effortless passage deeper into the chasm, and sleep.

The next time Claire opened her eyes, the room was in daylight, a powerful incandescence made even more dazzling by the brilliant yellow of the maples outside the window. David Preisler sat cross-legged on the other side of the room, reading a newspaper.

"What day is it?" Her throat, dry as wood, creaked with the words.

David looked up and smiled, then put down the paper. "It's Wednesday. Nearly noon. Don't worry, you haven't lost another day. You're right on schedule. How are you feeling?"

She wasn't sure how to answer, aware as she was of some new uneasiness. Not physical. Something else, vague and dreadful. She turned her head as slowly as she could to look about the room, then moved to position herself a bit higher against the pillow, but slumped back under the band of painful bruises and strained muscles encircling her chest and ribs. She tried to push up with her legs, but their aching stiffness defeated that maneuver as well.

David hurried over. "Hey, hold on there." He adjusted the pillows behind her back. "Better?"

"Better."

He gestured toward the open drapes. "Hope you don't mind. I thought you might like feeling the sun. It's a beautiful day." He picked up the small stack of magazines from the table at the foot of the bed. "Thought you might like these—McCall's, Redbook, Ladies Home Journal. Might be an interesting article or two in between the Minute Rice and toothpaste ads."

"Thank you, David."

He poured some water into the little green plastic hospital cup.

Claire took a sip, then leaned back on the pillow.

"You had a rough time of it last night. Gomshay says bad dreams aren't unusual after something as traumatic as a car accident, especially one like yours."

A bad dream? Is that what it was? A dream so real that she couldn't breathe? She squirmed. What was she trying to remember? She looked toward the closet. *Something happened last night. What was it, exactly? Yes. Yes …*

"What's wrong?"

She raised her arm feebly and pointed to the closet.

David turned to where Claire was pointing. "What is it?"

Her mind sped like a bumper car, darting, crashing—a man, a closet door, scattered pillows, drowning, a struggle to breathe. Suffocation. He had to have been hiding. Was that a crazy idea? About as crazy as drowning in bed. She lay back, grappling with a new fear—the realization of a new deadly encounter, and most definitely intentional.

"Hey, you're trembling. What's going on? Let me help you."

"David." The word came out like a moan. She felt so much weaker this morning. The effects of the sedative? The fight for her life? She could feel her face pulsating, flushed.

"Claire, I'm here. Let me help."

"Last night. It was no dream, David. The driver. He was here. In this room. He … he tried to kill me. He tried to smother me … with these bed pillows."

Preisler patted her hand, then pointed toward the window. "Look at what today has brought. Bright sunshine. Beautiful autumn color. That's real." He looked down at her. "These bad dreams will pass, Claire. They will."

"No, David." She struggled to sit up but couldn't. "That was no bad dream. He was here. I'd know him anywhere. He put the pillows over my head and held me down. I couldn't breathe. I was suffocating."

He adjusted her pillows. "Here, let's get you more comfortable. You're going to be fine, I promise. Nobody knows better than Dr. Gomshay. You just relax, and let me go get him."

She took hold of his hand. "David, listen. He hid in the closet. I saw him sneak out after the nurse left the room. I saw him."

"Let me get Doctor Gomshay. He can—"

"Okay. All right. But before you do that, please, just look in the closet."

Preisler stared at her for a moment, thoughtful. She could tell he doubted everything she was telling him.

She squeezed his hand. "Please."

"All right." His voice was calm. "I'll check. Just … just don't get yourself excited."

She lay there limp and breathless as David walked over to the large wood-grained door and pulled it wide open for Claire to see inside. The plaid wool dress that she had been wearing when they brought her in hung on one side, freshly laundered. A few more hangers were visible at the other end of the bar. Small white garments were set, neatly folded, on the shelf above, likely her underwear, while her one sling-back pump lay on its side at the back. There appeared to be nothing else. David reached down, placed the shoe right side up, turned to Claire, and shrugged.

"See? Just your clothes and your one beautiful shoe. When you're ready, we'll get some new ones." He closed the closet door and walked back to the bed with a smile that Claire guessed was intended to be reassuring. It was not. He sat on the edge of the bed and took her hand. "Look, you've suffered trauma from a terrible chain of events. You've had medication, which is likely still affecting you. Not only that, but you're in completely unfamiliar surroundings—perfect for someone's mind to start playing tricks on them."

Although she appreciated his trying to console her with reason, she was not comforted by his words. She didn't know which was worse—that someone might have attempted to kill her or that her senses had become so warped by the ordeal that she could have conjured up such a terrifying scenario. She pressed her eyes shut for an instant, confused and afraid. "David, please don't say anything to the doctor. To anyone. I'll be okay." She wasn't sure that she believed that. What she did believe was that sometimes things that are so credible, so certain, in the privacy of the mind, become ridiculous and untenable when they hit the air. Still …

"I know you'll be okay, but I really think we should let Dr. Gomshay know what's happened. You may have had a reaction to the medication."

"You mean I might have had a hallucination."

"Actually, it would be good news, wouldn't it? I mean, better than believing someone's trying to do you in." He gave a slight laugh.

She humored him by doing the same, knowing that there was a question she had to ask but, she had no intention of asking him or Dr. Gomshay. It would only continue to stir things up.

"I think I'll get some rest now." She was grateful when Preisler agreed. After he left, she lay back quietly, letting some time pass to be sure he was gone. Then, she buzzed the nurse's station and asked for Nurse Foge, one of the two from the night before.

"Your shoe? Oh, yes," said Foge, "I put it there myself yesterday afternoon, not that there's anything you're going to be able to do with just one shoe." The nurse shook her head. "It was absolutely caked with mud and soaked. You poor thing." She gestured toward the closet. "It cleaned up pretty well, however useless it might be."

She appeared to be a good-natured, robust woman of about fifty or so, Claire guessed, overweight but well-proportioned so that her uniform fit her stocky frame impeccably. She had curly light brown hair, warm intelligent eyes, and a wonderful husky laugh. Her face, which bore no make-up that Claire could tell, appeared kind.

"Do you remember how you put the shoe in the closet?" Claire asked.

Nurse Foge gave Claire a quizzical look, perhaps not so much to consider the answer as the question itself. "How?"

"I mean, did you place it there? You know … maybe just casually drop it in? I'm not saying this to be critical, I promise. So, please don't be offended. I'm asking for a particular reason."

Careful, Claire thought. Crazy questions don't go over so well. She was thinking a bit more clearly now, relieved to have finally shaken off the drowsiness from the sedative. Or might that be an illusion, too. Nevertheless, she did not want to be doped up again.

Nurse Foge squinted pensively, put a hand to her chin, and tapped her lip.

"I imagine you're thinking these questions sound … odd," Claire said. "Believe me, it has nothing to do with the condition of my one silly shoe. As a matter of fact, it was very considerate of you and the others to have done all you did. Thank you." Was she only digging herself in deeper?

"Right about now," Nurse Foge said with deliberation, "you're probably thinking that a simple question you've needed to ask for one reason or another has turned into a piece of crazy-sounding interrogation. And you imagine I'm thinking, 'Is she loony?' Am I right?" They laughed.

Claire felt both embarrassed and relieved by the woman's frankness.

"I've been a nurse for twenty years, Miss Fournaris. I've learned that those little questions, the ones that sound crazy or trivial, are very important to the patient doing the asking. What matters is that I answer them as respectfully as I possibly can. Your question happens to be one of the easier ones. The other night, a woman down the hall asked if we sometimes put more than one patient in a bed if the hospital gets crowded. A man once asked if it was true that the hospital wheelchairs have square wheels so the patients can't get away. So, don't worry about it. Let me show you." She walked to the closet and opened the door. "See, it's just the way I put it in." She bent down, presumably to add a convincing touch, and picked up Claire's sling back with one hand, hooking a finger through the strap. She held the shoe up for Claire to see. "I put it down just like this," she said, bending over to carefully place the shoe on the closet floor, toe pointing to the back wall.

Exactly as David had just done, Claire thought. "And what about my dress?" she said, struggling to lean on one elbow. "Did you put the dress in there, too?"

"All nice and laundered, just like you see," Miss Foge said, sliding the hanger to the center of the rod."

"Would anyone have reason to go into the closet after that? Do you think anyone did?"

Nurse Foge narrowed her eyes. "Is something of yours missing?"

"Oh, no. Nothing like that."

"Because if that's the case, don't hesitate to speak up. We've never had a problem with that sort of thing, but there can always be a first time."

"Nothing's missing. I was just wondering about whether anyone else might have gone into the closet for something."

"No one. These closets are hardly ever used. The patients usually can't get to them, the staff doesn't bother with them, the cleaning people check them out when they're here, and there have been no cleaning people in this room since you arrived. So, who's left?"

Claire felt a shiver. Who, indeed?

Chapter Four

THERE WAS NO doubt in Claire's mind that someone had been hiding in the closet. Earlier that day, when David opened the closet door at Claire's desperate insistence, the shoe was at the back of the closet. The dress was not centered on the rod but pushed to one side. Was it not clear to anyone else that things in the closet were out of place because someone had been in there?

That she had not begun losing her faculties was a comfort to her. That someone might wish to cause her great harm worked at her insides like the pinch of hot tweezers. She was worried and fearful. Still, she refused to panic as she had earlier. What she needed to do was get hold of Lieutenant Desiata without letting Dr. Gomshay or David know. They would think she was still having delusions, and that would mean only one thing— more medication. But she intended to have none of it. What she needed was to keep a clear head. And that could mean the difference between life and death.

At five that afternoon, Claire awakened from a nap following an arduous stroll in the hospital corridor using a walker, and had just been served her first full meal—tough roast beef with salty gravy and green beans that had suffered from too long in the steamer tray. She was pushing the food about unenthusiastically when she looked up and saw a man standing in the doorway holding a small wicker picnic basket.

He walked toward her. "Marjorie was right. She said that if we had to rely on your getting nourishment from the hospital food, you might never get well enough to come home." He extended his hand. "I'm Paul Farrow. It's possible you don't remember me."

This tall, well-dressed, roughly elegant stranger was no more what she had expected than anything else had been so far—not a trace of the puckish, sometimes horsey countenance of his slightly older sister, but … what? "I'm very happy to see you again. I was quite young the last time we met." She pulled herself higher against the pillow as best she could, suddenly very conscious of her appearance. It occurred to her that she hadn't once looked in the mirror. The nurses had seen to her hygiene and comfort, but she hadn't any make-up and thought that by now her hair must be as stringy as the fringe of an old floor runner.

"You've had quite a time of it," Farrow said. He had already moved her supper tray to the other side of the room and was setting the contents of the wicker basket before her on the rolling bed table.

He was tall and unsmiling, an athletic-looking man with light brown hair that blended with the shade of his camel sport jacket, his eyes dark and intense. As he moved about, Claire thought she caught Evelyn in a certain squareness of shoulder, some fleeting expression about the mouth, though he was far more attractive than his sister.

"I did come to see you before this," he said, "but certainly not as attentive as I should have been." He stopped and looked straight at her. "I'm finishing up an important project, a twenty-story building I've been working on for months. The developer was heading out of the country on other business, and the only time we had for an important phone call was, of course, the time of your arrival. I hope you'll forgive me."

"There's nothing to forgive. Honestly. I've been out of it a lot, anyway. But thank you for the visits and the flowers. Peonies are my favorite."

Having set the last small plate in front of her, he picked up the fork and spoon he'd laid on a yellow gingham napkin and handed them to her. "Marjorie was explicit about my seeing that you eat everything she sent, although I can't imagine how you could."

Evelyn had spoken of Marjorie with great affection on numerous occasions and had, for a while, at least, after every visit to her brother's, fallen into the habit of comparing nearly everything she ate to a similar, far superior dish that Marjorie had prepared. Claire could see that this spread would have met with Evelyn's approval—a delicate cream of cucumber soup, sliced chicken turnovers in flaky pastry, an iceberg wedge with tomato zucchini vinaigrette, lemon mousse for dessert. He was right; there was no way Claire could finish it all, but as much of it as she could consume was sheer heaven. "Please give

Marjorie my great thanks. This is very kind of her … and you. And I have to say, it's the best thing I've tasted in a very long time."

It was the oddest feeling—this paradox of meeting a person who is at once no less than your mother's brother, your only living relative, and no more than any other unfamiliar face that turns up beside you on a crowded uptown bus.

"Gomshay says you're doing better. I hope that's true. How are you feeling?"

"Stiff, but otherwise fine, especially now that they've eased up on the medications that made me woozy. And the nurses do get me up and moving, which I know is for my own good, taxing as it is."

He still hadn't smiled and seemed to be studying her, which made her uncomfortable. For lack of anything else to say, she went back to talking about how good the food was. She had expected that they would have more to talk about on the occasion of what was, more or less, their first meeting. Instead, there were moments of silence that neither of them seemed to know what to do with.

"Has there been any word about the driver?" she said, at last.

"Who?" He was clearly distracted. "Oh, the driver. So sorry. No, nothing yet, sad to say." He looked toward the window where the rapid onset of twilight had dimmed the brilliant yellow of the maples. "Would you like these closed?" he asked, and when she said yes, he drew the drapes. Then, he turned on a table lamp and returned to the bed, where he packed up the plates, wrapping the leftovers in the coverings Marjorie had provided, and placed them into the basket. "We can dispose of these at home. No point leaving more for the nurses to do." He was indeed hard to figure out—courteous, distant, polite, thoughtful, ill at ease. Cold.

The door opened, and the teenage volunteer in the Candy Striper smock who had delivered Claire's supper tray came in, shrugged shyly, then quickly appeared bewildered by the switch in menus and supper dishes. Farrow directed the girl to the table across the room where she picked up the tray with great relief, as if she had just been saved from the scandal of having lost the hospital property in her charge. As the girl departed, Farrow gave her an understanding smile, a pleasant transformation that might have warmed Claire's heart had it not revealed that her uncle was quite capable of being genial, with whom he wished.

"Thank you again for everything," Claire said to him, having no inclination whatsoever to add the word "Uncle."

"If there's anything you need, anything at all, we'll be happy to get it for you. Lyle … Dr. Gomshay … tells us you should be ready to be released on Friday. David can come for you, of course."

Of course—David.

He picked up the basket and went to the door, then turned. "I should have said this sooner. I'm sorry about Evelyn. About not making it to the funeral. I wish I could have been there. Truly."

"I understand," she said, not quite meaning it. "By the way, David's been very kind and helpful, but I think I'm causing him too much time away from his work. I'm sorry to have become such a nuisance."

"There's no reason at all for you to feel that way. What happened to you could happen to anyone. We want to help in any way we can."

We. Always we. Or us. It was increasingly apparent to Claire that, whether by design or nature, the apple of her aunt Evelyn's eye was a most impersonal gentleman, drawing a precise and careful line between them at the outset. Beyond the obligatory accommodations he might provide to any houseguest, there was likely not to be any gesture of avuncular endearment. Well, so be it.

"I was thinking," she said. "Under the circumstances, it might be better if I go directly home to Chicago when I leave the hospital."

He gave her a long, passive look and set the basket on a chair. "Are you sure that's a good idea? I don't know what kind of support you have at home. You may not be able to do everything for yourself for a while—shop, cook. Drive."

It surprised her that he would even think of that. "I have friends who can help out."

"Also, you did come here to settle some business."

How foolish of her. What was she thinking? She had become so preoccupied with her situation that she'd completely forgotten the reason for her trip in the first place. "Yes … well, of course. I mean … I can call the attorneys in Manhattan and see if we can arrange to put things off for a month or so, then return to New York when I'm fully recovered." She was careful to say New York and not Connecticut. "I can fly in for just a day or two. Shouldn't take much longer than that to sign whatever it is I have to sign. I don't see it as a problem."

He ran his hand across the back of his neck. "I'm not sure Lieutenant Desiata would agree."

She leaned up as best she could on one elbow. "What do you mean?"

"He's still investigating the accident, and, as far as we know, there's a person still unaccounted for."

Something else that had momentarily slipped her mind, but it did provide the opportunity she was looking for. "Would you do me a favor, please? Would you ask the lieutenant if I could speak with him? Maybe I can fill in some details that I was unable to provide when they first brought me in."

"I will," he said. "And there is one more thing. Marjorie suggested a small dinner party on the weekend. Nothing fancy or formal. Just a chance to meet people who knew and loved your aunt as much as we did."

Things were suddenly getting more complicated with a tangle of people she had no appetite for meeting right now.

"Meantime, rest." And without waiting for her response, he picked up the basket and left the room.

Chapter Five

THE NEXT DAY, Dr. Gomshay stopped by on his rounds. Claire was sitting up in bed, a task she had strained to finally accomplish without the aid of a nurse.

"And how are we doing today?"

"Much better, Doctor, but that's relative, I'd have to say." They laughed.

"And no more wrestling matches with the staff, I'm told."

"No more wrestling matches." How light people can make of things when they refuse to believe the worst.

He looked at her chart. "Good. You've had some exercise. The fitness of the body has a great deal to do with the fitness of the mind, and vice versa."

He was referring, no doubt, to the closet incident, and she resented it.

After checking Claire's vitals, he made notes on the chart and set it down. "And," he began with a self-satisfied look as if to conclude their visit on the highest of notes, "you've met your uncle." The doctor appeared to be more satisfied about it than she was?

"Yes, I have."

"Well?" Clearly, he was waiting for a grand endorsement.

"You seem to be very fond of him," she said.

"Everyone who knows your uncle is very fond of him. Oh, I mean, you know, of course, he's a low-profile fellow, reclusive in his own way." He waved his hand as though to brush off any negative implications of that truth. "Prefers a small circle of close friends and associates. Nevertheless, a true gentleman in every sense of the word. Decent, honorable. It's rare these days—a relatively young and very successful man with money *and* principles."

She had better offer something. "He brought me a lovely lunch. I'm sorry we never got to know each other as … well, you know … as family. But my aunt was extremely close to him."

"Ah, yes." He crimped his great pink brow. "Dear Evelyn."

"You knew her?"

"Oh, yes. Not well, of course. I had the pleasure of meeting her on more than one of her visits here. A fine woman." He shook his head. "The real tragedy of accidents—when one is lost who has so much life yet to live. Paul's not one to show his feelings, but he's still brooding."

"He did seem a little … distant."

"With you? That surprises me. I thought perhaps he'd open up, get some of that grief out of his system. He hasn't yet with any of us. But then, it is still only a month or so, and it's just like Paul not to want to burden anyone. He may come around once you're out at the house." He put his hand on hers. "Sharing your feelings of grief may be good for you as well."

Claire offered a weak smile, unable to imagine that she and Paul Farrow would be able to share much of anything on a personal level.

"Now cheer up, Claire. I've given permission for you to be discharged on Friday."

"I'm just afraid that my being at the house will be an imposition. As it is, Mr. Ettinger requires special care. How can I show up and expect people I don't know to start looking after me? It isn't right."

He frowned, dropping his eyebrows and mustache into great, wiry arches that transformed him into one of those endearing, forlorn creatures on a "Missing You" greeting card. "No need to worry, dear girl. Matthew Ettinger has his own nurse and his own accommodations. Now, as for you, just take it easy, and you will be able to do things for yourself, with some residual discomfort, of course." He wagged a finger. "But go slowly." He put his pen into the pocket of his white lab coat. "You're a strong woman, Claire Fournaris. I can tell. I saw it in your aunt. I see it in your uncle. A family trait, no doubt. For now, get your rest. If you feel you need a sedative, just ring for the nurse. Oh," he said, putting his finger to his lip." I understand you wanted to see Lieutenant Desiata. I hope we're not still going on about people hiding in closets."

People? No, just one. Possibly a killer! Had it really been necessary for her uncle to tell the doctor? She hated this sense of conspiracy that was taking hold in her. Why was everyone so caught up in the notion that she was imagining things, especially when it meant that her life might be in danger?

"Yes, actually, it was my uncle's idea." Two could play the same game. "He reminded me that the lieutenant needed to know more about the accident. Might as well do that as soon as possible while I still have a solid recollection of the details."

"Good. I believe he'll be here in the morning." Gomshay glanced at his pocket watch. "It's getting late. I'd better be on my way. There's a post-op appendectomy I've got to check on." He headed for the door. "Get a good night's sleep. It will help you put all those dark … things … in perspective."

When he was gone, she lay back, pondering the those "dark things" that he and, apparently, everyone else dismissed as delusions. The idea of resting appealed to her. Sleeping didn't. She intended to stay awake and on guard. She picked up the Saturday Evening Post, amused by the cover of a grandma trying to blow up her young grandson's football, then skimmed the pages, holding off as long as she could before it was impossible to take in one more line without nodding off. Still upright with pillows propped behind her and the nurse's call button held loosely in one hand, she reluctantly gave in to sleep, now and then waking briefly, scanning the room with eyes half closed to reassure herself all was okay, then dozing again.

By 7:45 in the morning, the blackness that had pressed itself against the large, curtained window had subsided. She moved slowly out of bed, made her way to the window, and pulled open the drapes to let in the first welcome light of day. On the street below, an elderly woman hurried along, her purse swinging from her wrist. A few people boarded the bus, while others got off, probably hospital visitors. She climbed back into bed, tossed two of her pillows onto the chair, and sprawled on her stomach, hungry for deep sleep, now only mildly aware of the soreness of her body.

At ten-thirty, Lieutenant Desiata arrived, and Claire's drowsiness gave way to relief that she might get somewhere convincing him about her nighttime intruder.

"I hope I didn't come too early," he said.

"No, it's fine. Thank you for coming, Lieutenant." There was something of the classic sleuth in him—a guy in a neat dark suit who follows the rules to the letter of the law until he doesn't, who likely shaves in his office after a long night on the job without sleep, always showing up late, if at all, to his family's Thanksgiving dinner, who instinctively knows the questions you have before you ask them, and whether the answers to his questions are true or not.

"I'm glad to see you're looking better than when they first brought you in." He turned to a fresh page in his small spiral notepad. "I understand there's more you might be able to tell me about what happened?"

She pressed her lips together. "Well, yes, and ..."

"And?"

"The truth is I've already told you all that I could recall." She jigged her position to sit straighter. "Lieutenant, I know everyone else around here thinks I'm delusional from the medication I was given, but I have to tell you there really was someone, a man, hiding in that closet." She leaned forward, pointing to the other side of the room. "It was blurry, but I'm sure it was the limo driver." She saw that Desiata had not written a word of it, but looked down at his notepad as if he might want her to think he would.

He didn't respond.

She forced herself higher on the bed. "You don't believe me. I was so sure you wouldn't be like the rest of them. You're the investigator. You're the one who should be following every single lead."

He sat taller in the chair, looked away, then turned back to her. "About the driver…"

Claire looked at him wide-eyed, attentive. Hopeful. "Yes?"

"His body was recovered late last night."

Claire gasped, covering her mouth with her hands.

"They found him trapped in a tangle of rushes about fifty feet farther along the shore from where they found you. It's clear that he'd been in the water for more than a day."

Claire dropped back against the pillows, staring straight ahead, unbelieving. "I just don't see how." She grabbed Desiata's sleeve. "I know what I saw. A tall dark figure in a long coat, someone you don't miss or mistake."

He dropped his shoulders and leaned in. "I know how hard this must be for you, Miss Fournaris …"

"No, wait. I have proof." She told him what Nurse Foge had said about the placement of the clothing, then she explained what happened when David opened the closet door with the shoe and the dress.

He tipped his head, as if recognizing some possible truth in what she was telling him. "And yet, we have the body, uniform and all."

"There's got to be another explanation."

"I'm not sure what that might be, Miss Fournaris. The driver is dead. This is your first time here. You're a stranger to everyone. Who would want to do you harm?"

"But that's it, I don't know. I…"

"You think I haven't paid attention. I have. You're here to sign papers relative to your aunt's estate. Your aunt was comfortable, but not wealthy. She had some assets but, clearly, not on the level her brother has enjoyed. So, if we were to look at a motive to kill someone for inheritance, that's out of the question, wouldn't you say? I seriously doubt that your uncle wants to do you in for his sister's bank account or mutual funds. It doesn't add up, does it?"

"Put like that, of course, it sounds ridiculous. Besides, that had never even occurred to me, although I appreciate your taking time to think of it."

"You said it best, Miss Fournaris. I'm an investigator. It's my job to think of it … every part of it."

She looked down, picking at her fingernail. "Makes me feel kind of foolish, but …" She looked him in the eye. "Someone, for whatever reason I do not know, had cause to hide in that closet and put these pillows over my head."

Desiata folded his notepad and slipped it into his side pocket. "What if it was a mistake? What if it was a kook with no connection to you at all? When you leave the hospital, why not try to leave that closet behind, too?"

She stared at him for a moment, then shrugged in reluctant agreement.

"But know this, Miss Fournaris. I can see how sincere you are. Let's just keep this conversation between us; don't mention it to anyone. And I mean not anyone—not your uncle, not Dr. Gomshay, not David Preisler. No one. Not even your nurse."

"Okay."

He got to his feet. "I will keep this on my radar, I promise."

"Thank you, Lieutenant," she said, brightening. "Thank you."

Later that afternoon, David Preisler walked in. She'd been sitting in the armchair by the window in a fresh hospital gown, the sunlight glistening warm on her still damp-combed hair. She had already taken her exercise stroll in the corridor and was feeling more limbered up than she'd felt in days, even though, mentally, she was still experiencing a somber confusion after learning of the driver's death.

"Well, now, that's much better," David said, with a broad grin.

She offered him a smile along with the chair next to hers at the window. Then, suddenly self-conscious about being caught more scantily dressed than when she had the benefit of bed covers, she reached for the pink satin robe her uncle had sent over by special messenger.

"I understand you'll be going home tomorrow."

"Yes, Dr. Gomshay told me."

"So, what do you think?" he asked.

"I'm happy to be getting out of here."

"No, I mean your uncle. What did you think of your uncle?"

She made a point of keeping a smile on her face. "We had a nice conversation. He brought me a delicious meal from Marjorie. He wanted to know if there was anything I needed. He was kind." She gestured to the robe. "He sent this. It's beautiful." She ran her hand along the sleeve. "He seems very generous."

David fingered the edge of the magazine he'd picked up off the chair. "Sounds like a neat little list. Is there a 'but' in there, somewhere?"

"Oh, I didn't mean to make it sound as though …"

"But…"

She hesitated. "I was telling Dr. Gomshay that my uncle does seem a little distant. Is he always so … I don't know … cool?

"He can be at times. More so lately since …"

"His sister's death? Dr. Gomshay says he's still brooding about it."

David looked off, squinting thoughtfully. "I'm not sure. I mean, it's only been a matter of weeks. I know he took it very hard. But there's something else, and I can't put my finger on it." He turned to look directly at her. "I really was sorry to hear about your aunt's passing. I don't know if I told you that."

He'd been sitting with his legs crossed, slightly slouched in the chair, confident, easy to talk to, the glint of sincerity never leaving his eyes. She could understand why her uncle, anyone for that matter, for whom it was vital to deal well with people, would want someone like David Preisler as an associate, a confidante.

"Thank you," she said.

He lightened again. "Now come on. Tell me. How are you feeling, really? What kind of night did you have? You look terrific."

She touched her hair, embarrassed by the compliment. "I had a pretty good night. The hot shower this morning was wonderful. Everything I've read about the healing power of water therapy is true. Only …"

He gave her a curious look. "Only?"

"I was surprised to find my stomach covered with scrapes and scratches. I don't see how they could have gotten there."

They turned when they heard the door open. Nurse Foge, a broad smile on her face, entered solidly in her thick-soled white shoes. "I wanted to catch you two before you left, David." She turned to Claire with a triumphant air about her. "The doctor is ready to discharge you today. Congratulations. He looked over your chart, got a good report from the night nurses, and from me." She winked. "He'll be here in a minute. He got waylaid coming down the hall."

"Oh, thank you, Nurse Foge. That's the best news I've had since … I don't know when."

David got to his feet. "You bet it's the best news."

While Claire still felt uncomfortable about going to her uncle's, she was glad to be leaving the whole closet ordeal behind. Maybe it was the medication, after all. In any case, she was now feeling more resilient, so much so that the misgivings she'd had after meeting Paul Farrow seemed less important, less real. And even if they weren't, she felt a bit more prepared to deal with her feelings, and with him.

Chapter Six

THEY MADE ONE stop before reaching the estate, a small pharmacy where Claire picked up some makeup items and a few other essentials. Then, finally, they passed through the wrought iron gate that led to a curved drive flanked by large tulip trees, and pulled up in front of the sprawling, two-story house.

It was an impressive place, less regal than Claire had imagined, but far more beautiful and welcoming with its pale gray granite stone, long sloping roof, and French windows and doors trimmed in white with black and white striped awnings.

No sooner had David stopped the car than the front door opened and a smiling older man with thinning red hair hurried down the front steps.

"Miss Fournaris, it's so good to have you here at last," said the man whose black trousers, vest, and starched white shirt with carefully rolled-up sleeves suggested, as did the place itself, an air of relaxed elegance. "I'm Roland Tarr, your uncle's butler. You can call me Tarr."

"I know of you from my aunt," she said, shaking his hand.

"We were all so happy when Mr. Preisler called from the hospital to say you'd be home today. May I help you with your things?" Then, apparently reminded of her predicament by the emptiness of the car, he added awkwardly, "That is, is there anything I can help you with?"

"Thank you, Tarr, but this is all there is." She gestured, almost apologetically, to the few small drug store parcels in her hand.

"Allow me, then." He took the packages from her. Then, he led the way into the house and through a spacious foyer to a sunlit room handsomely furnished in dark wood and overstuffed plaid chairs surrounding a fireplace. Lamplight and watercolors, French doors leading to a patio garden. It was the kind of earthy stylishness Claire had always pictured in a European country home.

On the far side of the great room stood a wide, angled staircase, where a vigorous- looking woman of about fifty hurried down the steps.

"Oh, there you are, Marjorie," David said. "I was beginning to wonder where you might be off to."

"Miss Fournaris," said Tarr, "I'd like you to meet Marjorie, Mr. Farrow's sometimes housekeeper, sometimes chef, and as you may already know, always my better half."

Yes, she did know. Evelyn had spoken of the pair with great affection. "I'm very happy to meet you, Marjorie," Claire said, stepping forward. "Thank you so much for the most amazing food I've had in a long time. A feast."

"Where is Mr. Farrow?" David asked.

"I believe he may still be in the study. The Professor stopped by, feeling a little better from his touch of ... well ... whatever it was," Marjorie turned back to Claire. "And I am so happy to meet you, too, Miss Fournaris. A lovely surprise that you would be released today. I'll have to apologize that we just found out. I would have hoped to do a bit more to make your arrival more enjoyable."

"Thank you, Marjorie, but I couldn't imagine what that might be. This is all so wonderful. And the food you sent to the hospital—honestly."

David headed toward the study. "Paul's with Arthur? Great! Glad the professor's on the mend."

"He's just home from the hospital and taking it slow," Marjorie said. "Louis had a touch of something himself, more like a slight head cold, really. But he's much better."

David took Claire's arm and led her toward the large double doors at the far end of the living room. "This is someone I believe you are really going to enjoy meeting, Professor Arthur Jakobiak."

"Evelyn mentioned him," Claire said. "She liked him very much."

"You bet. Great guy. Anthropologist, teacher, lecturer. And I have to say, a few of us thought … and you likely already know … that maybe Evelyn and Arthur might just have made something of their growing friendship."

"My aunt didn't say much about that. She could be very tight-lipped at times." Truth was that Evelyn had never mentioned it, but Claire knew that with Evelyn, anything was possible.

"He'll be at the dinner party," David said. "Paul did mention the dinner party, I hope."

Claire nodded.

"You'll also meet his daughter, Patrice." He dropped his voice to a whisper. "She's interested in your uncle."

"Ah." Claire gave him a sheepish grin. "And what about my uncle?" She whispered back. "Is he interested?"

"Hard to tell. They spend time together. Still, he keeps his distance, you might say."

The doors to the study opened just ahead of them, and Paul Farrow stepped out, a look of concern on his face. Behind him, Claire could see the French doors on the other side of the room standing open.

"David, good. You're here." Farrow took hold of David's arm, his voice quietly commanding. "Run up and get Parmalee, will you? Tell him I need him to take a ride with me over to Arthur's. He just left, nearly doubled over with stomach cramps again." He shook his head. "You know Arthur; I couldn't get him to wait for us to drive him. Said it was quicker to just take the shortcut home the way he came, through the woods. He looked pale."

"Stubborn as a mule," David said. "I'll get Parmalee."

Paul looked at Claire. "Seems I'm going to owe you another apology, but I hope you understand. There's something going round, and Arthur's not as young as he used to be."

"Please don't worry about me." She waved off his concern. "Everyone's been so nice, and I'm just happy to finally be here." It seemed strange to her that she meant it. Paul Farrow's home—this estate she had imagined would be daunting—was showing itself to be quite an agreeable place. She could see why Evelyn had spoken about it with great affection.

By the time David returned with Edmund Parmalee, the man Claire knew to be Matt Ettinger's nurse caretaker, Farrow had his overcoat and fedora on. "My niece, Claire," he said to Parmalee, by way of hurried introduction.

Edmund Parmalee was a solid man in the taut white uniform of his caretaker role. "Nice to meet you, Miss Fournaris," he said, as Tarr helped him on with his overcoat.

"I've already phoned Gomshay," Farrow said. "I figured it couldn't hurt for us to be up there until he arrives." He turned to Tarr. "You can keep an eye on Matthew; we won't be long. Marjorie, why don't you go ahead and show my niece to her room."

"Good idea," Marjorie said, leading the way to the staircase. "I do hope the professor will be all right," she called back.

"Not to worry," said Parmalee. "We'll do what we can."

Claire's bedroom was located on the second floor, as were all guestrooms and bedrooms in the Farrow residence, with the exception of Marjorie and Roland Tarr's quarters, located on the ground floor adjacent to one of the two south patios.

Marjorie hurried ahead like a child eager to spring a surprise or share a treasure, knowing that Claire would enjoy the large sunny room set in pink and white dogwood blossoms and soft floral prints.

Claire found it breathtaking and immediately felt at ease there. The wall containing the fireplace was otherwise nearly completely lined with bookshelves before which a sofa and armchair were set at a right angle facing the hearth. At either end of the bookshelves was a pair of French doors leading to a terrace that ran the length of the room. Claire could imagine herself catching up on much-needed sleep during the brief time she would spend there.

Marjorie placed Claire's parcels on the vanity, and with a self-assured smile, paused for what Claire guessed was a rare moment of immobility, apparently to enjoy the younger woman's appreciation of the setting.

"Thank you, Marjorie," she said. "This is a beautiful room."

"Oh, don't thank me," the woman said, with girlish modesty. "It's all to your uncle's credit."

"What's he like?"

"Everything your lovely Evelyn must have told you about him is true. Your aunt adored him. He's a fine man. On the quiet side. Kind. Generous. Rollie and I have been with Mr. Farrow and Mr. Ettinger since your uncle bought this estate about nine years ago, I guess it is." She gave Claire a sad look, pressing her lips together. "So sorry about your Aunt Evelyn."

"My aunt spoke of you with great affection, Marjorie."

"Then you also know, of course, about poor Mr. Ettinger. By the way, we always address him as Teddy. He relates best to that name."

About a decade or so earlier, according to the late Evelyn Farrow, Matthew Ettinger had been a happily married man living in Washington, D.C., aged thirty, successful architect and proud father of a young daughter, Bess. He was also a good friend and colleague of Paul Farrow, himself a successful architect, residing in nearby Virginia.

One day, while the Ettingers were on vacation out West, Mrs. Ettinger and Bess were killed in an accident. Ettinger himself was not injured. Heartbroken by the tragedy, and having no other family, he leaned desperately on his friendship with Farrow, who so worried about his friend's well-being that he urged him to move into his suburban Virginia home with him until he got back on his feet.

Ettinger reluctantly agreed, but his depression worsened. Within the year, still grieving, he suffered a massive stroke. Farrow, a bachelor, took upon himself the care and support of his friend, even to the extent that they moved to Connecticut in the hope that the pastoral and less hectic setting might aid Ettinger's recovery.

"Ah," said Marjorie, "you would have heard all about it from Evelyn." She sighed and shook her head. "There was a special lady, rest her soul. Wasn't enough she could do for all of us when she came."

A noise from behind the two women drew their attention to the open bedroom door where a tall, timid-looking boy, whom Claire took to be about seventeen, stood holding a toolbox and clearing his throat.

"I'm finished now, Aunt Marjorie."

"Oh, Bobby." She turned to Claire. "This is my nephew, Bobby Tarr. He helps his uncle and me with some of the odd jobs, and quite a hand he is at fixing things." The affection in Marjorie's words sounded genuine. Still, Claire detected a certain uneasiness in the woman's manner.

"Bobby, say hello to Miss Fournaris, Mr. Farrow's niece."

At Claire's greeting, Bobby Tarr haltingly nodded back a weak, shy smile, barely taking his eyes from the floor. "Pleased to meet you," he muttered.

Marjorie patted the boy on the arm and quietly instructed him to go downstairs and find his uncle. She'd be along shortly.

"He seems like a nice young man," Claire said.

"A nice young man who's still a boy, forgetful at times, and especially timid today, I see. And sometimes irresponsible in the most innocent of ways. But we do love him."

"I can see why." Claire touched Marjorie's arm. "I'm sure he must appreciate your patience with him."

Marjorie pulled her shoulders up into a deep shrug and gave Claire a tight little smile, as perhaps one appealing for understanding. A moment later, she gave the room a final look-over, followed by a confident air of approval, before departing.

When she was gone, Claire went to the bathroom to freshen up. The mirror she had used in the hospital bathroom with its harsh light that glared mercilessly off enamel walls had reflected the worst of her ordeal—her face, drawn and drained of color, dark lines like ruts beneath sullen brown eyes. Now, perhaps her high level of anxiety had put color back in her cheeks. She brushed her hair vigorously as if to do away with any recollection of the terrifying closet incident, but her mind was not at ease.

As she finished her light makeup routine with mascara, she couldn't help going over things in her head, all of it frightening. As much as others would prefer that she put the entire episode to rest, how could she? The driver's body had been found, but something was amiss, and while realizing that she was better off not to keep mentioning it, she was also not about to dismiss or ignore the fact that someone was most definitely interested in doing away with her.

She returned to the bedroom and took a seat in one of the comfortable club chairs by the French doors that led to the terrace, noticing for the first time the view of the woods and a glimpse of the front-door approach with its curve of driveway edged in cobblestones. Claire pulled open the doors and stepped out. The brisk October afternoon presented a natural gallery of trees and shrubs, deciduous and evergreen, many in varying stages of fall color from striking yellows to burnt orange. By contrast, great sturdy pines and arbor vitae, spreading yews and junipers stood like sentinels, less spectacular perhaps, but reliably verdant, ready to take the landscape through the otherwise colorless winter ahead. She closed her eyes to the distant scent of leaf burn before a faint tapping brought her back inside. She went to the door and opened it to see Paul Farrow standing there, unsmiling.

"Sorry again for the abrupt departure," he said. "How are you feeling?"

"Better, thank you. I believe it truly helps to be in such a lovely home." That truth wasn't going to stop her from leaving just as soon as her business was conducted. She stepped aside for him to enter.

"Marjorie thought you might enjoy having this room." He turned to survey the setting. "Evelyn had mentioned that you like pink."

"I do. And it is a beautiful room."

"Good. Glad you like it."

"How's your friend? I hope he's okay."

"His blood pressure was elevated, but the medics didn't see any cause for worry, except that he's got to take it slow. Arthur is pretty upset about spoiling your arrival."

"What happened, exactly?"

Farrow shrugged. "We were having a cup of tea in the study. He was talkative as he always is, going on about some find in the Middle East. Some ancient relic. He seemed okay. Then, next thing I knew, he was doubled over in his chair. Right now, though, I think Marjorie feels worse than he does—she's sure she must have let the tea steep too long."

"I hope she isn't blaming herself for Louis, too. I understand he had a touch of something."

"Something's going around," he said, rubbing the back of his neck. "You can always count on it once the first hard chill is in the air. But Louis is fine. I think they'll both—"

A flash of upward movement caught Claire's eye. She pivoted in alarm to see a large cat with thick fur the color of smoke land noiselessly on top of one of the bookshelves near the fireplace.

"It's okay." Farrow looked up at the cat. "Normandy! Come down!"

The sleepy-eyed feline settled in where afternoon shadows had created a cozy, darkened corner. Farrow gave Claire an apologetic shrug that she found amusing.

"This room is so rarely used," he said. "I guess he's come to think of it as his own."

"That's a generous attitude for someone who doesn't like cats," Claire said. "Evelyn mentioned it."

Farrow appeared a little self-conscious, as if possibly embarrassed by Claire knowing something about him he wouldn't have thought she knew. "Before you give me too much credit, I should tell you that Normandy is Matt's, and, as Evelyn might also have told you, it's never difficult for me to make concessions where Matt's concerned."

She was thinking how the passing years had deepened his voice, and wondered if it was ever pitched in laughter as his sister's so often had been.

He went to the door. "You should rest. We'll be having dinner at 7:00. Marjorie can bring you something now if you like."

"Seven will be fine." She smiled agreeably.

"As for that dinner party—we've scheduled it for tomorrow night. Just a few close friends, as I said. People who met Evelyn and liked her very much. They would like to meet you. And the cheerful gathering might help take your mind off things."

"It sounds very nice, except that I do have one small problem." She gestured to her clothing.

Farrow nodded soberly. "I've already made arrangements for Louis to take you first thing in the morning. Charge whatever you buy to my account."

"Only if you promise to let me repay you as soon as I can get some money transferred from my bank in Chicago."

"I can't promise that. And you need clothes. See you at dinner." He shut the door quietly behind him.

Claire slipped off her shoes and lay on the bed, sinking into the fullness of the comforter, still unable to figure out this uncle of hers.

CHAPTER SEVEN

THE CLOCK ON the bedside table radio said 3:40. She tuned in to a station with soft music as afternoon shadows, like long, soothing fingers, began to massage the jagged edges of sunlight that sliced the room. She didn't know what time it felt like or what day for that matter, only that it was most certainly the oddest of times—something Aunt Evelyn would have gleefully ascribed to the perplexing vagaries of life.

Normandy's sleepy eyes blinked at her from his high bookshelf perch. But Claire wasn't at all sleepy. She got up, crossed the room, and turned on the floor lamp in the corner, observing upon closer inspection that although many of the book titles were technical, along with perhaps even heavier subject matter such as Einstein, Machiavelli, and Jung, there were a good many current novels, among them, "For Whom the Bell Tolls," and "A Tree Grows in Brooklyn." She had heard so much about "Gone with the Wind," but couldn't imagine reading it in this state of mind. Nor would she touch any of the Agatha Christie's. *Murder? No thank you.* She decided to stick with her magazines for now, and climbed back into bed with a copy of "The Women's Home Companion." She had not intended to sleep, but once settled into the bed's quilted thickness, surrounded by the dreamy music and the comforting glow of the fireplace, she yielded.

When Claire opened her eyes, she was momentarily seized by disorientation, then fear. The room was in total darkness except for the illuminated clock face on the table radio—9:45. She groped for the lamp and welcomed the room's cheery pinkness. A lightweight quilt now covered her. She got up slowly, easing stiff muscles, and went to the fireplace where a tray containing a teapot and a covered dish were set on a long, low table. Normandy was gone.

Claire's stomach grumbled as if small depth charges were going off inside her. But she was quickly satisfied with the sliced chicken sandwiches and pot of warm tea. When she had finished, she freshened up, then carried the tray downstairs, hoping there was still someone awake to whom she could offer her apologies for missing dinner.

The house was quiet. A lucky guess brought her into the kitchen through a door at the far end of a short private corridor off the great room. A muscular man in white shirt and trousers stood at the sink, measuring a thick, clear liquid into a glass. Parmalee.

He stood, offering Claire a courteous nod and a broad smile that revealed perfectly even teeth, which, except for the single apparent flaw of a space too wide in front, were like the rest of him, straight and strong-looking.

"How is Mr. Ettinger?"

"He has his good days and his bad," said Parmalee, with little expression. He looked at her. "What about yourself? You had quite a close brush."

"Better, thanks." She thought of the driver, his fate still haunting her. "Is there anything I can do to help while I'm here … sit with Mr. Ettinger maybe?"

"That's very nice of you to offer, but it would take great patience. He—"

"Ah, there you are now," said Marjorie, hurrying in through the kitchen door. "Did you have a nice rest? Your uncle is in the study with Mr. Preisler. Come, I'll show you."

Claire and Parmalee exchanged amused shrugs. Then, feeling like an obedient child, Claire followed Marjorie to the room with the double doors at the far end of the living room. A telephone's muted ring sounded twice, then stopped. Claire wondered who would be calling so late; it was past ten.

The study, a large, Cyprus-paneled room furnished with comfortable club chairs and bookshelves, felt as welcoming as the rest of the house. David Preisler sat before the large stone fireplace, cigarette in hand. He smiled and stood when Claire entered. Marjorie had already scurried off to parts unknown, leaving Claire to wonder if people ever slept.

"Sleeping Beauty," David teased.

Under different circumstances, she would still consider him a bit of a stranger, but here among so many unfamiliar faces, she was very much aware that he was the friend whose company and kindnesses in the hospital filled those first vague and fearful stirrings of consciousness.

Near a windowed corner, Paul Farrow stood at a large, solid-looking cherry desk talking quietly on the telephone. As Claire approached, he placed the receiver on the desk, and went through another pair of double doors to a room David would later refer to as Farrow's private study.

"You'll have to excuse me for a few minutes," he said to Claire on the way. Then, to David, "I'll take this inside."

"I think I've intruded."

"Not at all," David said in an almost playful tone, as if sensing her awkwardness.

She was beginning to see that he was the pleasant, less serious counterpart to her uncle's often intense demeanor.

"Your uncle always prefers to take his calls in there."

"I guess I'm just a little surprised by all of the late-night activity."

"I imagine most people would be." He walked to a decorative side table that held a variety of decanters. "Now, what can I get you? A little cream sherry? Sambuca?"

She opted for the cream sherry and took a seat by the fire. Since waking, she'd felt a chill that the warmth of this room quickly abated. "Thanks," she said, accepting the glass from David. "Do you live here?"

"It seems that way sometimes," he said, amused, then took a seat opposite her. "I have an apartment in town, about twenty minutes from here. This is where we work. If we've worked late or if there's something special going on, like tonight, with you coming here and all, I stay over. My room is across from yours."

She felt comfortable there with him. He was easy to talk to, easy to get along with. She couldn't imagine any of this having worked out so well if she'd only had her uncle to rely upon. "What is it that you do exactly? If you don't mind my asking."

"I handle most of your uncle's business affairs. And Matt's. Your uncle's is pretty much the real estate end, residential designs. Matt's work was more about commercial properties that offer a variety of tax shelter options to investors, a particular specialty of mine. Just because Matt is on the sidelines doesn't mean his business affairs are."

"My aunt didn't talk much about her brother's business. Or Matt's."

"Tell me a little about you," he said. "What do you like to do back in Chicago?"

"Well, I'm very involved with my students' work at the college. I like to make sure they learn the most they can and do their best. Sounds boring, I'm sure. I also belong to a Canasta club. I play a little tennis, like to go to the movies. I just saw 'The Grapes of Wrath.' A bit heavy. So was 'Rebecca.' I should have known—Alfred Hitchcock. But 'The Philadelphia Story' was a lot of fun. Who doesn't love Cary Grant and Jimmy Stewart?"

"Maybe we'll see a movie together, before you leave," he said.

The doors to the private study opened, and Paul Farrow came back into the room, closing the doors behind him. He hung up the receiver, then gave a quick smile, as if suddenly realizing how serious he must appear, though his eyes remained dark, troubled perhaps, Claire thought.

"Is anything wrong?" she asked. *Please, God, let there be nothing more that has gone wrong.*

"Just routine."

David stood and clapped his hands together as Farrow poured himself a small Sherry. "Okay, tomorrow's agenda. What's the plan?" He made a little half turn on one heel to point himself in Farrow's direction. "So, you've told her about the dinner party tomorrow night. Good start."

"Better than that," Claire said. "He's even offered to have Louis take me shopping in the morning."

"Why don't you tag along, David?" Farrow said.

"Please." Claire put her hand up. "I don't see how I can let you do that. You've already spent too much time babysitting me."

Even as she protested, she felt relieved at having David's company, and hoped they wouldn't take her refusal seriously.

"We can spare him a while longer," Farrow said. "And I suggest you think about having David go with you to Manhattan …when you're ready. Do you have a firm appointment yet with your aunt's attorneys?"

How odd that he would refer to his sister as "your aunt"— once again putting distance between himself and people who should be close to him, family. "I was planning to call them tomorrow to set it up. I doubt that I'll be able to get there before Monday. When I spoke to them last week on the phone, they said that it shouldn't take any time at all to sign the papers and tie up all the loose ends."

"Good," David said. "Then it's settled—shopping tomorrow, then off to Manhattan on Monday."

Claire gave them a timid smile. "I really can't thank you enough. Both of you. And I haven't even apologized yet for sleeping through dinner. It doesn't seem possible to get so exhausted from doing so little."

Farrow gave her a wry smile. "I don't think you can call what you've been through 'so little.' And you're probably going to experience a bit of exhaustion a while longer as your body … and your mental state … recover."

David took a sip of his drink and placed his glass on the table tray. "Gomshay says rest and relaxation are what you need. And, right now, it's time I got a little R and R of my own. It's been a long day, and we've got another full one tomorrow." He looked directly at Claire. "Which I am definitely looking forward to."

When David had left the room, Farrow took a seat in a chair by the fire, leaning forward to rest his arms on his knees, thoughtful.

"Please don't stay up on my account," Claire said. She had nearly added "Uncle" but wasn't quite ready to call him that. He was still too much a stranger, and there was something awkward about saying it to someone who wasn't all that much older than she was.

"I'm really sorry about Evelyn," he said at last, without looking up. The remark came so unexpectedly and sounded so much like an appeal that Claire remembered at once what Dr. Gomshay had said about her uncle keeping his pain inside. She wondered if he was offering an invitation of sorts to commiserate.

"I know."

"Can you tell me anything about Evelyn's accident?"

"Nothing more than I had told you over the phone. She was in Cincinnati for a week. A convention. She must have spoken of it last time she was here."

He looked up at Claire. "Yes, she did tell me about it. She was excited."

"It's nearly all she talked about for weeks, since she had chaired the organizing committee. Anyway, the third morning of the convention, she didn't show up for breakfast. They checked her room and found her on the floor." Claire took a deep breath, looking away. "She'd hit her head against the corner of the night table. The drapery cord was looped around her ankle, apparently causing her to stumble."

Farrow sat listening, a grim look on his face. "I hope you understand how bad I felt not being able to come out to Chicago for the funeral. Tarr had my bag packed the night you called. I was planning to fly out the next morning, but out of nowhere I was hit with the worst flu of my life. Fever, dizziness, all of it. One of those miserable end-of-summer bugs that don't let up on you. I telephoned you a dozen or more times, but there was never an answer."

"It was a bad time for me. I went to stay with friends. But I did get your telegram explaining. It was left with my landlady." She set her glass down on the table beside her. "It was a lovely service. I think you would have approved. So many of her friends came. You'd probably remember a few of them—Glen and Alice Ferber, Ben Gerrardo."

Farrow's eyes searched the room as if to find the distant memory. "It's been a long time."

"Well, I was always grateful that you were able to make it back for my mother's funeral. It was so long ago, of course, but a terrible time, and I'm sorry to say I don't remember you very much or nearly anyone else. I was young and so shattered."

"Yes. Sometimes, grief and loss end up overpowering everything else, don't they?"

It was a time Claire would never forget. She was only nine. Her father, suffering with his own grief and loss after the agonizing eight months of his wife's terminal illness, made it clear that there was no way he could deal with the needs of a nine-year-old girl. "Thank God for Aunt Evelyn. It didn't take much for her to convince my father that it would be best if he allowed me to stay with her for a while. He did." She hesitated. "I never saw him again."

Farrow gave her a long look. "I'm so sorry about all that." He stood slowly and went to the fireplace, where he drew back the mesh screen and spread the chalky gray ash with the brass poker, sending up dots of fire that snapped to life and died away all in the same instant. He was clearly deep in thought, a serious figure made more somber by the darkness of his crouching silhouette against the blackened hearth.

"Evelyn spoke of you so often," Claire said, testing unknown waters for a swirl of current that she hoped would not throw her off balance. It was only a half truth. There was a time when Evelyn spoke often of her brother, remembering him as she had loved to from years past, the dynamic student, the young sailor, the maverick architect with the self-possessing spirit. In the few years or so before her death, however, she had come to speak less and less frequently of him. Claire never knew why. "She liked coming here." What Claire couldn't say was that Evelyn had returned from her more recent visits with a remote air about her, saying little, except for occasional references to the lovely people or events that had occupied her time, and only then, Claire felt, to put up a convincing show to her niece that she most certainly did have a 'delightful time' in Connecticut.

Farrow remained silent. He got to his feet slowly and turned as if about to say something. Claire wasn't certain what she saw in his eyes. It wasn't all sorrow. Pain possibly? If this was about losing Evelyn, well then, what about Claire's pain? Losing Evelyn was worse than losing her mother. Although she loved her mother dearly, she was young enough when her mother died that there had hardly been time to develop the kind of close, caring, irreplaceable relationship she later came to share with her aunt over many years. Didn't it occur to Paul Farrow to consider Claire's pain? Maybe she was being too harsh a judge, but it seemed that her uncle was most generous at giving what was easiest to give, the things that cost him only his money. But what if it were something else behind his moodiness? Something that had nothing at all to do with Evelyn? She held back as long as she could. "Is something wrong? Are you okay?"

"It's getting late," he said as he turned to pick up a few papers from one of the tables.

"I'm sorry," she said. "I didn't even think to ask how your friend is doing."

"Arthur? He might have some rough days ahead. Gomshay can't tell right now exactly what's taken hold. He's going to schedule a few tests once Arthur is strong enough to handle it. For now, lots of bed rest. Thanks for asking. And," he said, hesitating, "I didn't know if I should mention it. That was Lieutenant Desiata on the phone when you came in. He told me about the driver."

Claire cast her eyes down and said nothing.

"I'm sure that must weigh heavily. I'm sorry."

"It does," Claire said. "I haven't been able to get it out of my mind."

"I can imagine." He pressed his lips together, and for a moment, no one spoke. "Maybe these next few days … you know … keeping busy, meeting different people, the dinner party, maybe things will lighten up for you." He gestured to the fireplace. "Would you like me to put on another log?"

"No, it's okay. I'll be going back up soon. But thank you." She looked around. "It's a lovely room. Very comfortable even without the fire."

"I hope you get a good night's rest, Claire. See you in the morning."

Hearing him say her name for the very first time had an almost startling effect, as if it were some rarely spoken, ancient cryptonym. After he had closed the doors behind him, Claire fell back against the chair with a sigh. Paul Farrow was certainly too complicated to figure out. She was glad to glimpse his kindness, but in a few days, she'd be done with the legal formalities she had traveled east to take care of. She would finish her business, return home, and put all this behind her.

Chapter Eight

It was nearly midnight, but there was no possibility for sleep after the nap she'd had earlier. She sat for a brief time before the fireplace, watching the flames gradually fade to the tiny red dots that snapped one after the other, until there was only a black tuft of lifeless ash. She decided to return to her room to read. The house was still and silent when she emerged from the study and made her way up the staircase past several impressive still lifes and landscapes cast with a mellow radiance from the delicate etched glass wall sconces.

Her uncle was right. Things were weighing heavily on her, but it wasn't all about the limousine driver. There was still the terrifying thought—not at all a dream or a hallucination—that someone hiding in the hospital room closet had tried to suffocate her in her bed. She wouldn't have dared mention it again to Farrow or anyone, and that made the weight heavier.

As she passed the second-floor sitting room, she heard a man's voice, speaking in a slow, steady stream of words, although she couldn't hear what was being said. There was no other voice that she could hear. Claire paused in the hallway to listen and quickly guessed that the voice was Edmund Parmalee's. She now also knew who the silent member of the conversation must be. The door was slightly ajar. She knocked quietly, and Edmund Parmalee's low voice called for her to come in.

Still in his caretaker whites, Parmalee sat across the room facing a wheelchair whose occupant Claire was unable to see. Parmalee stood when Claire entered. "Teddy is with me, Miss Fournaris. Why don't you come and meet him?"

Claire hesitated, not wanting to intrude the way she had earlier in her uncle's study, but Parmalee beckoned with a wave of his hand. Like the rest of the house, the room was a comfortable, softly-lit setting where Parmalee sat in one of two armchairs next to a handsome side-table holding a brass lamp and a small stack of magazines.

As she approached, she saw a ghostly white hand resting almost lifeless on the wheelchair's black padded arm. Oddly, it was not a frail hand as one might have expected, but sinewy and strong-looking.

"Claire Fournaris, I'd like you to meet Teddy."

"Hello, Teddy."

Parmalee turned the wheelchair and reached forward, gently tapping Ettinger's hand, as if to awaken him. Ettinger, dressed in blue pajamas, was not asleep, although his gray-green eyes, watery and half-opened, appeared transfixed upon some random point in middle-distance. His hair, dark brown and thinning at the top, was neatly trimmed and combed back, his mouth drooping slightly to one side.

Seeing this sadly debilitated man, whom she knew to be only in his forties, it struck Claire that, except for the darkness of his hair, he looked like a man playing the part of a much older one, the way she remembered the drama students doing in the plays back at college, only far more convincingly.

"Please don't disturb him," she said. "It's late. Let him rest."

"The hour has little to do with it. He's on his own clock."

"I understand." She took a step closer. "I'm happy to meet you at last, Teddy. I know of your great talent as an architect."

"Did you hear that, Ted? She's an admirer."

There was no response, only the limpid stare from hollow eyes.

Claire looked at Parmalee as if in appeal.

"You reminded me of your aunt just then," he said. "She would become so involved, then more disappointed when I couldn't say he'd done something marvelous that day or showed some miraculous sign of improvement. She was a very caring woman, Evelyn was."

"Thank you." She looked at Ettinger in silence as she rose to leave.

Parmalee got up and walked her to the door. "Sometimes he's better than this, sometimes worse."

"Does he hear the things that are said?" she whispered. "Does he understand?"

"There are rare times when he not only hears and understands but even attempts to respond with a word or a sound blurted out that I can only interpret as frustration. Yet

…" Parmalee looked over at Ettinger. "There are times when it seems he might lift himself from that chair, though I can't imagine how he could."

"What about when he's like this?"

"Sometimes tremors. Otherwise, mostly this way." Parmalee shrugged. "Who knows—from all appearances, I might just as well be speaking to a garage door. But he's not a garage door, Miss Fournaris, is he? He's a human being. And the moment I forget that, then I am truly in a worse state than he is."

Claire touched Parmalee's arm, then turned to look at the slumped figure that hadn't moved. "My aunt sometimes returned from her visits here quiet and preoccupied. I never knew why. But I will say that she was impressed by you, Mr. Parmalee."

Back in her room a few minutes later, Claire was unable to get Matthew Ettinger out of her thoughts. His gaunt, white visage hounded her sympathies while reinforcing the unsettling truth of these last few days—there is, after all, a frighteningly thin line between life's routine and that single extraordinary event, that solitary moment, that bears in its meteoric swiftness the stunning onset of one's destiny.

Marjorie had been there. The bed was neatly turned down, beckoning Claire with its soft pink satin sheets and pillow cases edged with fine white scallops. A nightgown lay across the bed. She changed into it and rinsed out the few items she would have to put back on in a matter of hours, sure that Marjorie would be able to dry them for her when the time came.

She picked up McCall's magazine and propped herself up in bed with pillows, but after leafing through page after page, she knew that she was too unsettled to read. She found some notepaper in the drawer of the night stand and started jotting a list of things she must remember to do: check in back home with her landlady, jot down all the items her uncle had bought for her so she could repay him, call her colleagues to see what was going on at the college. Since taking a sabbatical following Evelyn's death, she checked in with her fellow professors and some students once a week. But, right now, there was too much swirling about in her head. She looked again at the clock—nearly one. She put down the notepaper and turned over, trying to stretch out, but her stomach was still too tender from the mysterious scratches she'd noticed earlier that day in the hospital shower.

The wind had picked up. She'd heard it come in waves, breaching the night-silence of the surrounding woods with a soft rush that swelled as if to separate limb from tree and maybe even tree from earth. Then the windows rattled, and branches scratched and clawed the house before the next brief silence. She was accustomed to Chicago's wicked winters. Now, here was autumn in New England—bone chill and ripping wind. Even so, Claire felt comfortable and warm. Too warm perhaps to sleep. The room, restful and inviting when she had entered, now seemed a little stuffy, something she decided to remedy by opening wide one of the French doors for a moment's dose of October air—just enough to make her delight in crawling under the bed quilt.

She put on the terry robe, pulled open one of the doors, and stepped out onto the balcony where it appeared that a great black drape had fallen over the world. The wind was a refreshing swirl that billowed her gown and sent her hair in all directions. Even the large potted shrubs set along the wall, thick with vines, appeared ready to be yanked out by their roots. Clutching her robe tight around her, she closed her eyes and took a deep breath.

As the roar of the wind mounted, Claire felt a strange exhilaration as if at this moment she were the only human being privy to some cosmic marvel. Gradually, her eyes adjusted, making it possible for her to discern in the darkness beyond the rail the noisy sway of trees, dense and ominous, while all at once she and everything around her were in a windswept frenzy. She closed her eyes against the leaves that flew at her like bats, her exhilaration suddenly tinged with apprehension.

As she turned to go back inside, a tangle of vines caught her ankle. Then, where the inky darkness was ever so slightly diluted by the weak spill of light from her room, she saw him. Amid the windswept evergreens, a singularly menacing figure in the surrounding fury, arms outstretched, reaching for her.

Her scream, swallowed up in the roar of the wind, did nothing to deter her assailant. In his powerful grip, she was forced backward toward the railing. Her ankle still caught in the curl of vines, her step faltered, and his grip momentarily loosened. She twisted wildly until she managed to face the railing and grab on tight, throwing her head forward between her outstretched arms to brace herself.

All at once, the wind subsided, and she could hear the labored grunts of her attacker along with her own whimpering gasps as he seized her by the hair and pulled her head back. He banged her head against the rail, forcing her to lose her hold. Knowing that it would only be an instant before he tossed her off the terrace to her death, she bellowed one long, shrill protest that tore from her throat. He was lifting her now as she struggled wildly in his grasp, her ankle still caught. When he suddenly let go, Claire fell backward noticing, as her assailant must have, that a light had been turned on. There were voices. People calling. Someone was coming. Marjorie!

Claire lay there exhausted and breathless as the woman put her arm under Claire's shoulders, gently cradling her. "Oh, my dear. My sweet dear."

Then David was there. "Good grief! What's happened?" Tarr was behind him. All were in their pajamas and bathrobes.

"I'll go for compresses," Tarr said.

"She got her foot tangled up in some vines, poor thing," Marjorie said.

David walked around to the other side, where Claire lay, and looked at Marjorie. "I've got her." He scooped Claire up in his arms, carried her inside, and placed her on the bed. "Are you okay?" He carefully moved back the hair from Claire's forehead. "You've got quite a bruise. What on earth happened?"

"Looks like she took a bad spill," Marjorie said.

"No!" Claire shook her head with a slow sweeping motion, gasping between sobs. "It was him again."

"Him?" Marjorie looked at David.

The bedroom door opened, and Paul Farrow came in, followed by Parmalee, both also in their night clothes.

"She seems to have had a bad fall," David said.

Parmalee moved quickly to Claire's side to check her vitals. He looked at her pupils along with the bluish mound that was surfacing at the top of her forehead just below the hairline.

"Is she all right?" Farrow asked. "How did this happen?"

Parmalee looked up. "Nothing to worry about. A nasty bump, though. It will likely be sore for a while. An ice pack should help bring it down."

"Rollie's gone for one," Marjorie said.

David gestured to the terrace. "Looks like she got her foot caught in one of the vines and fell against the railing,"

Farrow rubbed the back of his neck. "What on earth was she doing out on the terrace on a night like this?"

Claire drew a deep breath, her face flushed and tear-streaked. "Listen to me. Please!" She spoke slowly, making every effort to keep her voice even and controlled. "I did not fall against the rail. I was pushed against it." She tried to sit up. "By the taxi driver. The taxi driver! Do you understand? The same man who tried to kill me in the hospital."

"Great glory be," Marjorie muttered.

"He was trying to kill me by throwing me over the railing, but my foot was caught."

"Claire," David said, "don't do this to yourself again."

"If my foot had not been snagged by that vine," she went on with deliberation, making eye contact with each of them in turn, "he would have succeeded in throwing me over the rail."

"Claire, please …"

"No, David. Stop. Please," she said. "He is real. He was here, and it's clear now, that whoever he is, he intends to kill me and will not give up until he succeeds."

Marjorie gasped. "But how is that possible? Who would do such a thing?"

Farrow shot Marjorie a look of stern caution, and for the moment, no one said a word, as each looked at the other in disbelief. Tarr, who had returned with the ice packs just in time to hear Claire's account, listened, dumbstruck.

Farrow took the ice packs and handed them to Marjorie, who applied them gently to Claire's head. He then turned to David. "What is she talking about?"

David hesitated. "In the hospital, she …" He looked at the others, then at Claire, as if to seek her approval for what he might have to reveal. Claire knew he was remembering the promise he'd made to her about not telling anyone of her hysteria and of the terrifying closet event.

"Tell them, David," Claire said without looking up.

David glanced again at the others. "Would you mind excusing us for a few minutes?"

"Not at all," said Parmalee. Then he, Tarr, and Marjorie left the room, shutting the door quietly behind them.

Farrow looked at David. "What's going on?"

David began again, but Claire interrupted, holding the pack against her forehead. "Let me, David." She looked up at her uncle. "Two nights ago, in my hospital room, something happened to me while I was sleeping. It was as if I was back in the car, going down under water, unable to escape or to breathe. The nurses came running in. Doctor Gomshay said it was a nightmare. They found me hanging out of bed, gasping for breath, my bed pillows scattered on the floor. Afterwards, just before I fell back to sleep, I saw a man come out of my closet and leave the room. The room was very dimly lit, but there was something about him. I would have sworn it was the driver of The Village taxi. The next day, when I woke up, I felt troubled and wasn't sure why, but as my head cleared, I realized that it was no dream—that man had tried to smother me."

"Claire …"

Claire put up her hand before Farrow could comment, and went on. "I was frantic, nearly out of my head with fear. I didn't dare tell the doctor because all he would do was give me more medication. I needed to be clear-headed. I told David in confidence, and he helped me see that I was likely all wrong, that it was a natural thing to have bouts of wild imaginings because of the car accident. He managed to convince me." She looked at David. "Mostly. I had to agree that the whole thing sounded preposterous. Still, deep down, I wasn't convinced.

But I made David promise not to tell anyone how hysterical I'd acted." She drew a deep breath, adjusting the ice pack. "It had all been too real to me. I questioned the nurse about the things in my closet."

David shook his head. "But, Claire, we went over all that." He turned to Farrow. "She asked me to search the closet. I found nothing."

Claire rested the ice pack on the towel in her lap. "You thought you'd found nothing, David, but you were wrong, and I didn't let on. You remember that my shoe was lying on its side at the back of the closet, and you straightened it?"

"Yes, but what …"

"When I asked the nurse, she said my clothing and that shoe had been placed in there neatly; she'd put them there herself. But the shoe was at the back of the closet, and the clothes hanger was pushed to one side. You straightened it, remember? Someone had been in that closet."

"Claire, listen to me—"

"But even at that, David, I was willing to put that whole crazy scene behind me. Doubts and all. Fears and all. Until tonight."

Farrow had pulled over a chair and sat beside the bed. "What exactly happened tonight?" His voice had a gentle earnestness she hadn't heard before.

"It was warm in the room. I wasn't sleepy. I went out on the terrace. The air was refreshing at first. Then, the wind whipped up again and just as I turned to go inside …" She pressed her eyes shut and felt her body shudder. "This dark figure … this menacing figure … came at me and tried to push me over the rail. Luckily, the wind must have blown the vines around, and my foot got tangled up in one of them. That's probably what saved me. When he realized it was difficult to shove me over the rail, he banged my head against it instead. He was lifting me up just as the lights came on."

Farrow looked at David, then back at Claire. "But you never saw his face?"

"No. It was too dark." She straightened up. "They found the driver's body. I don't know what to make of that. All I know is that the same person who tried to kill me in the hospital is the same person who tried again tonight. And he's the same person who drove the limousine taxi."

Farrow leaned forward, resting his elbows on his knees. "I'm very sorry about all this, Claire. I had no idea. I promise we'll get to the bottom of it. But I do know that Leonard Kimmons drove for the limousine company for nearly twenty years. I knew him well these last many years as a very decent family man. So, you can imagine how puzzling this is." He got up and walked over to the terrace doors, flipped the light switch, and pulled the doors open. The wind tore at him from all sides. He looked about, then came back inside. Claire was thinking how strong and in control he seemed at all times and how he, too, must be doubting her story. She could feel frustration building in her, but was resigned not to allow her emotions to take over and threaten her credibility.

"One of the large arbor vitae is down," Farrow said calmly as he closed the doors and clicked the deadbolt. "Tipped over in its pot." He brushed his hair back with his hand and straightened his robe.

"Claire," David said, "isn't it possible that … well, in the darkness …"

"Oh, yes, David," Claire snapped, "you must be right. In the darkness, this large potted plant grabbed me by the arms, dragged me across the terrace, pulled me by the hair, and banged my head against the railing. That's it, of course."

David looked at Farrow, a look that Claire was beginning to recognize as a request for direction.

"I'll get hold of Desiata in the morning," Farrow said, as Claire exhaled with relief. "A crime has been committed. He'll need to come and evaluate everything. How did this guy get onto the terrace, for starters? There might be evidence. I'll call first thing."

Marjorie entered with fresh ice packs.

"Thank you, Marjorie," Claire said. "And thank you, Paul."

"Are you comfortable staying in this room tonight?" he asked. "I can have Tarr stay right outside your door. Or I can have Marjorie help you get comfortable in another room."

"I'd be happy to stay right here with you." Marjorie gestured to the recliner in the reading nook. "That's quite a comfortable chair."

"I think I'll be fine here. The door is bolted. I'll leave a light on. But thank you, Marjorie." Claire looked at her uncle. "And no need for Tarr. But thank you again."

Claire lay back as they exited the room, hopeful that her exhaustion would help her sleep. She reached for one of the magazines just as the bedroom door opened and Paul Farrow came back in.

He walked over to the bed, reached across Claire to pick up the ice pack, and handed it to her. "It won't do you any good over there," he said, without expression. He watched her as she applied the ice pack to her forehead with a nervous smile. Then, he turned and quietly left the room.

Claire lay there with the bewildering realization that she had just been ever so slightly comforted, while in the corridor Farrow took David aside.

"Remember when Arthur had to leave today and headed home through the woods?" Farrow whispered.

David nodded.

"He told me there was a man out there, in a heavy black coat, which is interesting, since the weather was not that cold earlier today."

"Who was he?"

"The fellow took off when Arthur spotted him."

"So … you think it's possible that—"

"Given what's happened, David, yes, I think it's possible."

Chapter Nine

The next afternoon, with Normandy eyeing her from his bookshelf perch, Claire stood before the full-length mirror in her room, holding up the jade silk dress she planned to wear to the dinner party still scheduled for eight that evening. The other items she purchased that morning now hung in the closet or occupied drawer space. Hard as she tried, none of it could take her mind off the horrifying incident the night before. Lieutenant Desiata had come while she and David were shopping. He had found nothing. The wind had taken care of whatever traces might have been left.

Claire stepped away from the mirror and dropped into a chair. There had been so much talk about who would want to kill her that no one seemed to be asking why. Why would someone want her dead? She had never been to this area. She had never met any of these people. Her business here had nothing to do with them. If a limousine driver wanted her dead, what would be his motive? The mantle clock caught her eye—nearly one-thirty. She would have to hurry to be back in time for the dinner party.

After pulling on a skirt and blouse from her new wardrobe, she made her way down the corridor, careful not to run into anyone. At the top of the stairs, she scanned below and seeing no one, hurried down, turning through the large arched entry and out of the house. Louis Joel would be waiting for her, but not in the drive directly outside the front door, as he had that morning, waiting for her and David. In a brief, private moment when she had seen Louis, she begged him to take her on an errand that no one else must know about.

Now, hurrying along the front of the house, she met him at the far end of the six-car garage where he was tucked out of sight in the bronze Jaguar he typically drove. He moved quickly to open the back door for Claire, and she noticed again his flawless posture and his perfectly tailored tan uniform, which gave his appearance a military aspect.

Claire was quick to express her gratitude, which he accepted with modesty and politeness, saying very little. Apparently in his mid-thirties or so, he had a look about him that suggested street-smart toughness with a hint of mischief. Yet, his almost regimental manner made it clear that he was well disciplined in the protocol of his job. This was her first opportunity to ask him about the details of the car accident, since he and David were the ones who rescued her.

"How long will it take to get there?" Claire asked him.

"Fifteen, twenty minutes."

"Since we have the time, Louis, do you mind if I ask you about the accident?"

"Sure. What do you want to know?"

"I'd like to hear your version of what happened."

He hesitated, catching her eye in the rear-view mirror. "Just like David said. We saw an odd flash of light ahead of us on the road, like maybe a car out of control. We found the spot, as best we could, where it went off the road and entered the woods. Actually, it wasn't that hard; there was some kind of reflector there."

"A reflector?"

"Yes. Bright, as though it marked the spot."

"That's strange. Don't you think?"

"For all we know, it might have created a distraction for the driver and caused him to lose control. Anyway, I eased the car off the road onto a kind of clearing that, we later found out, ran down through the woods all the way to the lake. We couldn't tell that at the time because it was pitch black. So, we got out and began making our way down, looking for the car. It never occurred to us that it had run right into the water. Eventually, we started calling out. That's when we heard a weak voice. That was you, Miss Fournaris. We pulled you out just in time."

"Pulled me out? You mean I was in the water?"

"Oh, yes."

Something didn't compute for Claire. "But I had made it to shore. I had pulled my way through the reeds until I collapsed on the bank. It was hard mud. I know I was not underwater."

"You were when we found you. It was David who grabbed hold of you and lifted you out of the water. He gave you mouth-to-mouth resuscitation."

Claire was shocked, hearing details she hadn't known before, details that didn't fit with her own flimsy recollection. One thing she was sure of—she was face down on nearly dry ground when she heard someone coming, someone she believed to be a rescuer. But the picture that Louis was painting showed her that someone else had been there first, a person who dragged her back into the water. It all made sense. "Louis, there was someone who got to me before you and David did. That person dragged me back into the water. That's why I have scratches on my stomach. Who else could have done that except the limousine driver?"

Louis talked to her through the mirror. "Wow. That's a terrifying thought."

"I want you to know that I'm very grateful for how you helped me that night."

"I'd say it was my pleasure, but you were very close to death, Miss Fournaris. There was no pleasure in seeing you that way. It was pretty awful."

"You're very kind, Louis. And please call me Claire." She looked out the window, then back, catching his eye again in the mirror. "So, tell me … if you care to … do you have family?"

"Just my parents. Out West. Oklahoma, to be exact. I see them a few times a year. They're good people. I can say the same about the people here on the estate. You probably know by now that David's assistant, Lucy Conant, and I have been going out. I guess it's been about a year. I'm very lucky."

Claire did not know, but it sounded like wonderful news. "I'm so happy to hear that, Louis. I believe I'll get to meet Lucy at the dinner party tonight."

As they got closer to town, Claire reached over and handed Louis a note with an address on it.

At the next stoplight, he looked at it. "This is a residential area. I thought you were going back to the shops where David took you yesterday."

Claire had told Louis that she needed to buy gifts for Paul, David and the others, but didn't want them to know. "I need to stop at this address first, if it's okay." She used a carefree tone, unsure as to how he would react if he knew her true mission. "It's all part of the secret," she said with a playful smirk.

Louis eyed her in the rear-view mirror with a sly grin. "No problem," he said, and the car gained speed.

One Eleven East Meadow was a white clapboard, split-level house in a neighborhood of once model-like homes and maple saplings set in place thirty years earlier, before the trees, as well as the houses themselves, all took root deep in the rich suburban soil, everything maintained—trimmed, mowed, and mulched. The October sky hung like a lumpy gray coverlet thrown over the cars packed bumper-to-bumper along both sides of the narrow street and side-by-side up the driveway belonging to the late Leonard Kimmons and his widow.

Claire wanted her arrival to be low-key. Since she doubted that was possible, pulling up in a chauffeur driven Jaguar, she asked Louis to drop her off on the next block and wait for her there. When she looked back a few minutes later, she saw that he had turned the car around to keep an eye on things, a gesture that gave her all the more reason to like him. He knew, by now, whose house it was; she didn't need to tell him. Nor had she said outright how uneasy she felt about coming. Yet, she sensed he knew that too. Just before she stepped from the car, he'd said, "Do what you have to do. I'll be right here."

At the entrance to the house, Claire found the front door wide open; only the glass storm door stood between her and the noisy gathering inside. She could see people clustered at the top of the short staircase in what was obviously the kitchen. Before she could ring the bell, a plump woman dressed in black noticed her, and with a sweetly sad expression on her face, came with slow purposefulness to open the door just enough to tactfully ask whom she could say was calling.

In as quiet a voice as possible, Claire gave her name. "I hope I'm not intruding. I just wanted to offer my condolences to Mrs. Kimmons." They both hesitated. "I'm … I was the passenger who …"

Before Claire could finish, the woman pressed her lips together and rolled her eyes, a look Claire perceived as an expression of dire apology. She then clasped Claire's two hands in hers. "I am so sorry. I'm Joan Fabrizi, Leonard's sister."

"My sincerest condolences, Joan."

"Please. Come." The woman led Claire up the few steps and across a living room filled with people sitting and standing around chatting amiably, many with small plates of food or glasses filled with one beverage or another. A few children wriggled past them, laughing, out of breath.

Claire was not at all comfortable knowing something dreadful about the deceased that would shock everyone in the house, something that even his widow was not aware of—that, in all likelihood, she had been married to a cold-blooded killer.

The décor was Italian provincial, everything done in blue, from plush pile carpeting to ornate cornices and heavy tie-back draperies. It struck Claire that the Kimmons's had done well for themselves.

At a right angle to the living room was the large dining room, where another dozen or so people sat or hovered around a long table set abundantly with platters of meats and casseroles, cheeses and breads, beverages, and desserts before a wall covered in photos and, in the center, a crucifix.

With Joan navigating, Claire shouldered her way to the far end of the table, where a woman with dark blond hair, appearing to be in her mid-forties or so, sat before a plate on which a single slice of baked ham lay untouched. The woman had a far-off look in her sad eyes and an inch-long curve of ash teetering at the end of the cigarette she balanced in her manicured hand.

Joan carefully removed the cigarette and pressed it into the heavy cut glass ashtray. "Louise." She spoke in a tone soft enough not to attract attention from the others.

The woman turned her face up with the bewildered look of one awakened too early from much-needed sleep.

"Louise." Joan took the woman's hand as if to signal the import of the moment. "This is Claire Fournaris, the woman who … who was in the car …"

It took a long moment before the twitch of the brow, the flicker of recognition showed on the woman's face. She stood with some effort and a feeble nod, her mouth quivering beneath eyes pooling with tears.

Claire extended her hand. "I hope I haven't intruded, Mrs. Kimmons. I just wanted to let you know how very sorry I am for your loss."

"Oh … yes," the woman said, slow, distracted, as if some essential, irretrievable part of her had been left far behind in another life. "Thank you … thank you … for coming."

Joan put her arm on Claire's. "I know this must be very hard for you." She gestured to the table fare. "Please. Sit. Have something to eat."

The last thing Claire could imagine was to sit and eat something, especially here, especially in this moment. For days, her world had been breaking off in chunks and falling about her. She wondered how many more pieces it would take before she was buried alive with suspicion, fear, and dread. Her face felt flushed, the back of her neck damp and prickly. Maybe she should sit for a moment. "Thank you, but I don't have much of an appetite."

"I … understand," the widow said, her voice half-choked.

Whether because it would have been awkward for Claire or for herself, the woman did not introduce Claire to anyone, but, almost apologetically, began with halting steps to lead Claire back across the living room, and up a short staircase where she stopped once to balance herself against the polished wooden handrail. Claire assumed they were on the floor where the bedrooms were located.

At the top step, the woman turned. "Would you mind … if I … if I spoke privately with you for a few minutes, Miss …?"

"Not at all. Claire Fournaris. Please call me Claire."

In a large room, which Claire presumed to be the master bedroom, the woman pointed to a chair for Claire to sit, then peeled away a few of the sweaters and lightweight coats belonging to her guests, and sat on the edge of the bed. "I know the accident must have been a terrible thing for you. Terrible," the woman said, eyeing Claire's forehead and the bluish bump Claire had attempted to conceal with make-up and a sweep of bangs.

Claire felt anxious. She wondered what the woman would think if she were suddenly to blurt out: *Oh, you mean this silly little bump? No, this bump was given to me by the poor dead man you're all mourning, who slammed my head against a terrace rail post even as he lay in his coffin.*

"I feel awkward asking …" The woman drew a deep breath as if taking in fuel for a rough trip ahead. "… but could you tell me … since you were the last person to … I mean … to see my Lenny … would you mind telling me what it was like? The accident?"

And for one more time, Claire churned up all the angst of that night, believing the woman had a right to hear the wretched details first-hand. What she suddenly realized, however, was that without the terrorizing particulars of Claire's ordeal following the accident, there wasn't really much to tell—the accident itself had happened without warning; the car swerved off the road into the blackness of the trees and barreled downhill into the water. The driver quickly vanished.

Mrs. Kimmons went on. "Did you talk … as he drove you? What did he say? He was such a friendly man. He loved to talk."

This came as a surprise. "He was quiet. Maybe he wasn't feeling well. Maybe that's why … why he might have lost control of the car."

The woman put her face in her hands and sobbed her words. "To die this way … just … just isn't right for my Lenny."

Claire reached over and tenuously put her hand on the woman's shoulder, even as feelings of guilt about her own survival stirred in her. "We don't know why these things happen, Mrs. Kimmons. I can only imagine how painful it is for you." And there was something else, of course—whatever anyone wanted to make of the closet incident in the hospital, there was simply no question that she had been attacked out on the terrace by the limousine driver, the man this sorrowful widow just buried. Claire shuddered and said nothing more. She had no words of comfort for the poor woman … or for herself. Nor could she make any sense at all of a single thing about it.

At one end of the dresser was a stack of what appeared to be leather-bound booklets. The one on top bearing the symbol of a crucifix embossed in gold. Claire recognized what must have been Mass offerings and memorial cards from the funeral parlor.

"He was always so thoughtful," Mrs. Kimmons said with a woeful smile. She had lifted her tear-swollen face and looked straight ahead as if stepping dreamily into her own past. "He helped everyone … anyone. There's a boy downstairs. Francis. A neighbor's boy. Lenny delivered him. Ten years ago. In a snowstorm. Now, we have two more days of his wake before his funeral Mass. We still have family coming from out of state. It all happened so fast."

Good Lord, Claire thought feverishly, what alternate reality is this? Those people downstairs are mourners. The rite of Christian burial. Nothing here could account for Claire's horrifying delusions or support even the vaguest possibility of their occurrence. Her heart ready to burst, pounding as it was with fear—the worst kind—fear of herself. Could she possibly be so wrong? But how?

The Jaguar was waiting. Louis Joel, properly expressionless, stepped out to open the back door and said nothing. Claire remained silent for a good while. She was fatigued, almost numb. It was not until they were nearly halfway home that one of them spoke.

"Bad?"

She nodded to him slowly in the mirror.

"I'll be glad to listen, if you need to talk about it … when you're ready."

"I didn't even go for the best reason—to pay respect to his widow." Her voice was even, dulled by mixed pains. "I didn't believe he was dead, Louis. I don't want to believe it." She looked out the window, then caught his eye again in the mirror. "It doesn't make sense that he is, does it?"

"Consider your circumstances," Louis said. "You've been through a lot."

"Do you know what those circumstances are, Louis? I'm not sure how much you know about everything that's happened."

He gave her a puzzled look. "I meant the accident."

"Yes, the accident," she said, trailing off. Had he been privy to the particulars? Had David shared them with him? Louis was another one who had become an instant friend of sorts, respectful of her predicament, sympathetic. Could she afford to tell him the things that might lead him to believe, as David did, that she was not quite in control of her faculties?

He kept eyeing her in the mirror, obviously waiting for further explanation.

"Have I missed something?"

"No," she said, her voice flat. "I'm just tired. Don't mind me." She slumped back in the seat and stared out the window, the bronzy woodland skimming past. Trees in full fall color. Now and then, a startling yellow. Some already bare. Here and there, a swirl of leaves joined the scattering that had already given up their hold. Another year nearly at its end. Soon 1941. Where were the years going? And what does any of it mean, anyway? She wished she was in the mood for beauty, for anything that would change the replay of her visit with the grieving Mrs. Kimmons.

Her thoughts, desultory at first, soon became methodical, like picking up a messy pile of index cards that had to be alphabetized. She went through the stack one at a time. House. People. Widow. Memorial cards. Photos. What was she looking for? House. People. Memorial cards. Something, but what, exactly? A pebble in the shoe, nagging, troubling. What was it? Coats and sweaters. Widow. Photos. *Wait!* Claire drew a deep breath and held it, not wanting to move, not wanting to jar the single wisp of logic that until now had fluttered past without notice. How could she not have thought of it sooner? She was just there in the house. How could she have missed it? How could she have missed the most obvious and telling of all things?

CHAPTER TEN

NEVER ASSUME ANYTHING, Aunt Evelyn used to say. Claire had allowed herself to make a careless omission, a single faulty presumption upon which all else was based—everything, right from the start. She straightened up and looked about eagerly, as if faced with a choice of ten roads to take and not knowing which direction to try first. But in truth, there was only one—the road back.

"Louis." She reached forward, pressing his shoulder. "Louis. Stop. We've got to go back."

"Go back?" He slowed the car.

"Yes. Yes. Please, Louis."

"Are you sure about this?"

"I'm sure. I … I forgot something." Then, she had to catch herself. "Oh, but … but only if it's okay. I mean, you've already been so kind. I don't want to get you in trouble."

"We're good." He chuckled. "Don't worry. You want to go back, we'll go back."

She had observed from the start an almost sly benevolence the way he accommodated David and Paul without sacrificing his own self-respect, managing to prevail with civility when there was more than one option on the table. He had clearly attained a level of high regard on the Paul Farrow team. How could she believe he was going to get in any trouble?

"Same as before?" he asked.

"Same as before. I don't think I'll be as long."

At a place in the road with a wide enough grassy shoulder, Louis pulled off and swung the Jaguar cautiously into a U-turn. The clock on the dashboard said 3:50 when he parked up the street from One-Eleven East Meadow and let Claire out for the second time that afternoon. The twilight sky was deepening to pewter, most of the cars that were in front of the house now gone.

As if needing no explanation, one of the guests came to the door and led Claire into the living room, now back in its proper order. Only a few others were there, putting   the finishing touches on the clean-up task and stacking the platters for tomorrow's use when the house would again be filled. Louise Kimmons came out of the kitchen, a bewildered look on her face. "I thought I heard your voice." She took Claire's hand. "Is everything all right? Did you forget something?"

"Could I please see you alone? Upstairs, where we spoke earlier?"

"Of course."

The bedroom, too, was now back in order. The stack of memorial cards remained, as did the photos.

"Please." Mrs. Kimmons her eyes were rimmed in red. "Why don't you sit and tell me what's on your mind?"

Claire didn't sit. She walked to the dresser where the photographs were lined up. "Would you mind if I looked at these?"

"Of course not." Louise squinted. "You came all the way back to look at the photographs?"

"Is your husband's picture here?" Claire asked.

"I can't believe you're asking me that." She walked over and gestured to the photos. "You can see that he's in all but two." She hesitated. "Oh, I'm sorry. Do you need to borrow my reading glasses? Forgive me."

"No, it's all right. Thank you, Louise. Sometimes, I just need a closer look at things."

"I understand."

Claire looked closer at the man who stood with his arm around Louise Kimmons in one of the photos. In the next photo, the same man with a group of volunteer firefighters. In another, alone in front of a Christmas tree in the corner of the downstairs living room. When Claire had first seen the photos earlier that day, she had been so preoccupied with seeing the face that wasn't there that she never gave a thought to the face that was. But why should she have? The man in these snapshots—the slightly stocky, round-faced man with the broad smile and jet-black hair—was someone Claire had never seen before in her life. Claire was sure that Louise Kimmons could hear her heartbeat.

The woman placed her hand on Claire's arm. "I can tell something is going on. Please tell me."

A million shards of thought blew through Claire's mind. Right now, only one, the least true of them, could be spoken out loud. "Nothing wrong, Louise. I'm so sorry for making you think there was. It's just that … well … I never really got to see your husband's face. It was very dark that night, and he'd been waiting in the car for me."

"In the car? That's odd. Lenny always liked getting out and meeting his passengers, taking their luggage, and so on."

"Well, it was a bit cold. And I could tell from his raspy voice that he must have been concerned about coming down with something."

Louise Kimmons turned her head to the side like someone quietly grappling with an unknown.

"The truth is," Claire went on, "your husband is someone I'll always remember in a very special way." She put her head down. "I'm a little embarrassed to ask." She clasped her hands together to keep them from trembling. "Do you have a photo of him that I might keep. After I left here today, it occurred to me that I might never have another opportunity to see what he looked like."

Louise Kimmons removed an embroidered handkerchief that she had tucked in her sleeve and pressed it to her eyes. After a moment, she opened the top drawer. Claire could see several stacks of photographs and other small mementos, before the woman removed a single snapshot of her husband.

"This was taken about a year ago, just about this time. We had so many sycamore leaves. They nearly covered the yard." She handed the photo to Claire.

And there he was, a man in a blue plaid long-sleeved shirt and khaki trousers, standing alone on the front lawn, dark-haired and smiling, an upright rake in his hand. There was enough definition in the sunlit face for Claire to see the well-shaped features of a strong, good-natured fellow, probably about five nine, looking no older than his mid-forties.

Claire took the photo. "This is wonderful, Louise." She reached over and hugged the woman. "Thank you so much. You have no idea what this means to me." Only later did it occur to Claire what this might also have meant to Louise Kimmons.

By now, night had settled in. The weighty overhang of trees that blocked even the light of the street lamps made it hard to spot the Jaguar, and no doubt hard for the Jaguar to spot her, but as she began making her way in the dark, she saw the car's lights flash, and a few moments later, the Jaguar rolled up.

Claire hurried to the car and jumped into the front seat. "Louis, listen to me." She was nearly breathless.

"Are you okay? Did something happen?"

"No. No. I mean, yes. I mean … listen. Louis, I've got to see that police lieutenant who's working on the accident. Will you take me?"

"Take you? Now?" Louis turned from her and grabbed the steering wheel with both hands. "It's 5:30. I've got to get you home for your uncle's party. It's for you, don't forget. And by now, they're probably already wondering where we've been all afternoon."

"What are you going to tell them?"

"Just that you'd forgotten a few things and asked if I'd take you back to town."

"Louis, this is important. I've just learned something about the accident. It's a little complicated. I can't go into it now. But I've got to tell that lieutenant something very important. It can't wait, Louis."

For a long moment he said nothing, his hands still fixed on the wheel. Claire was impatient. She turned, looking straight ahead. "Louis, I have to tell you." Her tone was both quiet and deliberate. "If you don't agree to take me, I intend to go back inside and call a cab."

The car still had not moved. Louis stepped effortlessly from the Jaguar and opened the passenger door. Claire's heart sank. The last thing she wanted to do was show up at the Kimmons's yet again, this time to call a cab.

Louis stood silently beside the open door.

Claire's anger flared because she knew something else now— she knew that David had indeed told Louis everything, or at least enough to convince him that she might try to pass off her delusions onto him. Why else would he disregard the urgency of her request to see the lieutenant?

Probably to his great surprise, Claire stepped from the car. "Thank you, Louis," she said, the chill of the night in her voice, as she began walking down the street in the direction of house number One-Eleven.

"All right. Come on!" Louis called out, his voice conciliatory.

Come on where, Claire wondered. She kept walking.

"I'll take you to Police Headquarters."

How could she be sure? Once she was back in the car with him at the wheel, she knew he would take her back to her uncle's. "Good night, Louis," she said without turning around. "Thank you for taking me here today. I want you to know I really do appreciate it."

"I said I'd take you. Isn't that what you want? Come on, get in. It's too cold and too dark for you to be walking around out here."

"Good night, Louis."

She was still walking when she heard the car door slam. A moment later, the Jaguar was rolling alongside her.

"What's the point of being so stubborn? Look, I was there. I saw David pull you out of the water. The driver was already gone. Drowned. You know that now. You met his widow. How much more proof do you need?"

"All I can say is there's a lot you don't know." Her voice was reaching fever pitch along with their tempers.

After a moment, the Jaguar drove off. Luckily, Claire hadn't yet reached the Kimmons's house. She turned and hurried back up the street. Halfway along the next block, she selected a well-lit house, telling the woman who answered the bell that her taxi had left before she realized she'd given him the wrong address.

With the generosity of a phone call, it didn't take long for a cab driver to pull up in front of the house. "Police Headquarters, please. And hurry."

CHAPTER ELEVEN

LIEUTENANT FRANK DESIATA sat in his shirt sleeves behind a plain, heavy wooden desk with its short, neat stacks of manila files and a scatter of loose papers. The whiteness of his shirt, vanishing as it did into the whiteness of the wall behind him, gave his stern, dark face an almost mystical quality, as though his head were hovering unconnected. "Good to see you again, Miss Fournaris," he said, rising from his chair. He looked at his watch. "But I have to say I'm surprised to see you at this hour." He gestured for her to sit.

"Thank you, Lieutenant. I'm so glad you're still here."

He gave her a curious look. "Are you alone?"

"Yes." She took a deep breath, then, referencing the water cooler just outside his door, asked if she could please have a cup of water. After accommodating her, Desiata sat back down at his desk and waited.

She emptied the small paper cup, not realizing how thirsty she had been, how dry her mouth had become from anxiety and lack of food—she hadn't eaten anything since breakfast. "Thank you, Lieutenant." She placed the empty cup on the edge of his desk. "I've just come from Louise Kimmons's house, and I have something extremely important to show you." She knew she shouldn't have been surprised that the lieutenant didn't even flinch at her news but just continued to sit there with his hands clasped in front of him.

"And what is that, Miss Fournaris?"

Claire reached into her purse, removed the snapshot, and passed it across to Desiata. "Lieutenant, do you know who this man is?"

He looked at the photograph. "Leonard Kimmons, the taxi driver."

"Who's taxi driver?" Claire said, a measure of triumph in her voice. "Not mine."

Now, at last. He flinched. "I don't follow you."

"Lieutenant, this may be Leonard Kimmons, but this is not the man who drove my limousine taxi on the night of the accident."

Desiata sat up. "Miss Fournaris, you strike me as an intelligent woman. You must be aware that the trauma resulting from an accident as severe as the one you had can—"

"Oh, yes, yes … could cause me to imagine this and that. I've heard it all, Lieutenant, but the simple truth is that until this afternoon, when I saw Leonard Kimmons's photographs on the dresser at his home, I had never set eyes upon this man in my entire life … ever."

"You went to his home?"

"Well … yes."

He was silent for a moment, appearing to process something he had not expected to hear. "How can you be so sure? Think about it. Wasn't it dark? How much of the driver did you actually see? I'm even wondering if you can be sure that it was a man."

Claire's certainty hadn't allowed for this thought. "He seemed to have the stature of a man … I mean … maybe not like a twenty-year-old, but it could have been. Mostly, a completely different body type from the shorter, solid-looking man in Louise Kimmons's photographs." She leaned forward. "Trust me—they are … two … different … people."

"So, let's see. You were in a limousine that had an accident. You were rescued, the driver was not. His body was later recovered from the lake where the accident occurred. He was identified as Leonard Kimmons. Now, you say that this man was not the same man who drove the limo." He ran his hand across the top of his head. "I have to ask you, Miss Fournaris—does this make any sense?"

"There's more." Claire shifted in her seat. "Louise Kimmons was quite surprised, Lieutenant, that her husband did not get out of the car to meet me and carry my bags to the limo, something that he always did. She seemed surprised that her husband didn't talk because of a raspy throat from a head cold. Apparently, her husband didn't have a head cold. I'm telling you—this was not her husband." She turned away in frustration, then faced him again. "And as for any of this making sense … well, it certainly makes more sense to me now than it did a few hours ago."

Desiata sat back in his chair, his dark eyes roving, thoughtful.

"David kept trying to convince me that everything was in my imagination." She waved her hands about. "The man in the hospital closet who tried to smother me, the man at my uncle's who tried to throw me over the terrace rail. Now, we have proof; there actually is another man."

"Why do you suppose this other man … this other person … let's say, possibly a woman, would want to kill you?"

"I have no idea. That's now the part that truly defies all logic. I didn't even know anyone when I arrived here. Not even my uncle. Well … not really." She folded her hands in her lap. "And you've just made it more complicated with this idea that it might have been a woman."

"Let me ask you. How do you think this person who was driving the limo taxi survived the accident?"

"I survived."

"You were very lucky. David Preisler pulled you out of the water just in time."

Claire reached over and laid her hand on his desk. "That's another thing. I had made it to the lake bank. I was no longer in the water." She pointed to her midriff. "I have scratches all over my stomach. Do you know where they came from? Someone dragged me back into the water."

"Let's see." Desiata removed the top folder from the stack to his immediate right and opened it. "The official report indicates you were removed from North Lake, administered resuscitation, and delivered by ambulance to the hospital, where you were admitted to emergency as a drowning victim." He looked at her, waiting for a reaction.

Strange, she thought, that this file, of all those on his desk, should have been the one sitting right on top at his very fingertips. She squinted. "You knew I was coming, didn't you?"

"Does it matter?"

"It matters if it means that they've told you I'm as mad as a loon, and you were convinced of it before I could tell you my side." She looked away, lips pressed together, anger rising. "Was it David? My uncle? Their trusted chauffeur, Mr. Joel?"

He started tapping a pencil nonchalantly on his desk blotter. "If I were inclined to think you were crazy, Miss Fournaris, I wouldn't have needed them to tell me—you've supplied me with enough to have formed that opinion on my own. If I were inclined, I said."

For a long moment, she stared across the desk at him very nearly detecting a grin, and in some odd way, feeling reassured.

"Try to put things in perspective," he said. "Your family is very concerned about you. It might be useful to you to believe that there is no conspiracy."

"But if they were really concerned, they'd be trying to help me get to the bottom of this, so that one of these days this … maniac … whoever he is … or she is … doesn't succeed. He's bound to try again."

"To kill you?"

"Yes," her voice wavered as tears welled, "to kill me."

"I have a suggestion." He came around and leaned against the desk, facing her. "As long as you're here, why not look through our mug shot books. Who knows, maybe something will come of it. When you're through, I'll drive you home."

Claire nodded her agreement. "What this means … and it's a horrifying thought. What this means, then, is that if Leonard Kimmons was not driving the limo, but was later found dead…" She took hold of the lieutenant's arm. "Then, Leonard Kimmons didn't drown at all. He was murdered."

Desiata put his hand over hers. "As bad as things sound, Miss Fournaris, let's not jump ahead. One thing at a time." He took her arm and led her to a room similar to his office. "Right now, all I want you to do is to look at photos. That's all. Sergeant Greeley will be here with you." And for the next hour and a half, she sat with the sergeant at a long table, turning page after page of photos, one unsavory character after another parading before her weary eyes. Her driver was not among them.

When Desiata dropped her off at the front door of her uncle's house, it was nearly nine. Tarr came hurrying to the door, more formally attired, and whispered, "Good so see you back, Miss Claire. They're in the living room."

As she approached, she heard the murmur of voices, both giddy and low-key, one in particular, a woman's slow, throaty laughter. Uncomfortable enough to even enter the room, late as she was, she realized that she hadn't so much as freshened her lipstick since leaving the house that afternoon. What must she look like? Instinctively, she brought her hand up to touch the tangle of her worst bird-nest look. All eyes on her now, she tucked her blouse into her waistband as her uncle stepped forward, wearing the tight smile of someone forcing himself to be gracious.

"Here's Claire now." He led her into the small group. "Some you already know," he said to her. "David, of course. Doctor Gomshay, Lyle, and Miriam."

She nodded. "Good to see you again, Doctor." She shook Miriam's hand. "Very nice to meet you."

"My niece, Claire Fournaris," he said, gesturing to others sitting about. "Bob and Hannah Lillian, good neighbors, good friends. Lucy Conant—David's assistant—a good friend, as well. You'll be seeing a lot of her. Bud Thomas … well, everyone here is a good friend. Patrice Jakobiak." He turned to Claire. "It was Patrice's father, Professor Jakobiak, who was taken ill here yesterday. Louis had also been down with something, but as you know, he recovered quickly."

She couldn't miss his facetious tone. "Oh, yes. Louis is better. I hope the professor is, too."

"I wish I could say he is," said Patrice Jakobiak.

"Sorry to hear that." Claire hesitated, looking about at the faces, smiling and expectant. "I have to apologize to all of you. Something came up that I had no choice but to take care of."

"Yes." David gave her a cool look. "Louis told us."

"No apologies necessary," said Miriam Gomshay, a tall, trim, athletic woman with a tasteful hint of lavender in her wavy, silver hair. "You've been through so much. It's a wonder you're even up and about. Besides, it gave us a little more time to relax and catch up. In any case, I'm very happy to meet you. Your Aunt Evelyn was a delight. I am so sorry for your loss. I feel it is very much ours as well. And I certainly hope your visit improves over what you've experienced so far."

"You've missed dinner," Farrow said, feigning, she was sure, a pleasant demeanor to which the others were likely somewhat accustomed, but not her. "However, we did wait on dessert."

"Oh, well, then," Claire said, almost timidly, "would you mind if I kept you waiting just a few minutes longer while I make myself presentable?"

"Not a bit." Bob Lillian, a tall, bulk of a man, about fifty, appeared as well- groomed as he was gracious. "Although I fail to see how you could hope to improve upon something that nature herself has made no mistakes with."

"Uh, oh!" Hannah Lillian laughed the loudest. "Better see that these two sit at opposite ends of the table."

Claire was halfway up the stairs, still trying to process this oddest of all predicaments—frivolity and murder—when she heard David call to her from the foyer. He followed her up.

"How the heck could you?" His anger was no less visible because of his whisper.

"I've offered my apologies. What I had to do just couldn't be put off."

"That whole business with the Kimmons's house? And giving Louis a hard time about coming home? Then, going to

Police Headquarters? How much crazier will you allow this to become?"

"There's been no craziness at all, David. Not from me, anyway. And that's not the only thing I discovered today. You should be happy for me."

"David." Paul Farrow had come up behind them on the stairs, his tone quiet but firm. "Don't let my niece keep our guests waiting any longer than necessary."

Claire continued on to her room, managing in a matter of minutes to throw off her clothes, freshen up, jump into the jade silk dress, then apply lipstick, along with a few subtle strokes of blush. This craziness was not over, not by a long shot.

CHAPTER TWELVE

DESSERT WAS ANOTHER of Marjorie's wonderful creations—gateau noisette, a light chocolate fluff with ground pecans between merengue layers, light as air. The dining room was a marvel of comfort and elegance—curves and color, warm woods, original art—plush hominess.

Hannah Lillian was the first to offer cheers. "I've been trying to lure Marjorie away from your uncle for ages."

"So have I." Patrice Jakobiak looked around the table with a sheepish grin. "But then I said to myself, if Marjorie won't come to me, I may just have to come to Marjorie." She raised an eyebrow in Paul Farrow's direction. "In a manner of speaking, of course."

Except for Claire, Farrow was the only one who didn't laugh, sitting there, instead, with a faint smile, fingering the stem of his wine glass from which he did not lift his eyes. Claire wondered if such a flirtation had ever been encouraged or, under different circumstances or surroundings, reciprocal. It was easy to understand what a woman like Patrice Jakobiak, or any woman for that matter, would see in Paul Farrow—money, position, influence. Claire wondered if it mattered very much to Professor Jakobiak's daughter that Paul Farrow was also handsome.

"Your aunt told us you're an English professor back in Chicago," Miriam Gomshay said. "And by the way, one of my favorite cities—Chicago."

"Mine too. I teach at a small private college, although I'm on sabbatical until the first of the year."

"Well, now I'm even more impressed," said Bob Lillian. He turned to Patrice. "Does Arthur know we now have another professor in our midst? And, by the way, you are certainly not like any crusty old professor of English that I ever saw."

"Will you be staying long enough to attend the Gala, Claire?" The friendly, girlish voice from across the table belonged to Lucy Conant. Like Patrice, Lucy was an attractive blond but without quite so much of the glamour."

"The gala?"

Hannah Lillian looked at Farrow. "Don't tell me you haven't told her, Paul. What are we going to do with you?" She turned to David. "And you're no better, my friend."

Farrow rubbed the back of his neck. "Sorry to say there's been so much going on around here, Hannah, that the last thing on my mind was the gala, wonderful as it always is."

"I doubt that I'll be able to attend in any event," Claire said. "I'll be leaving in a few days."

"Oh, please stay." Lucy Conant leaned in, a huge smile on her face. "It's only next weekend and such an important event, the annual hospital benefit. Miriam is this year's chairperson, so you can be sure it's going to be a fabulous time."

Patrice moved some bits around on her plate with a fork. "You'd really be missing out. Your uncle has promised to take me, but he's backed out of things before."

Hannah Lillian pressed her hands together, prayer-like. "Please come. We would all love to spend more time with you. And you wouldn't want to leave before meeting Arthur. Since he hasn't been on an archeological dig somewhere, he's been up to his ears overseeing every detail, as he usually is with all of his foundation work."

"That's probably why the man is so sick," Gomshay said. "He's run himself into the ground. He just won't let the volunteers do their part. He's got more than a hundred of them who want to help. Stubborn fool."

Claire glanced at her uncle, who had not looked once in her direction. Probably still stewing over what happened that day, she thought. "Thank you all so much. But as soon as my business here is finished, I'll have to get back to Chicago, probably by mid-week." So much small talk, she thought. So much inconsequential banter—galas and happy visits and sweet compliments. What did any of it have to do with the murder of an innocent man or the attempts on her own life, which not one person at the table appeared to know about or believe. She wondered how much longer she would be able to feign composure.

Patrice turned to Claire. "I hope you realize that my father will be very upset if you don't attend the gala. He told me to make sure you promise him at least one dance."

"I'm flattered," Claire said. "And I would like to know more about his foundation."

"An extremely worthwhile enterprise," Bud Thomas said. "It provides funding for critical disease research and treatment."

"Worthwhile as it is," Gomshay said, "a person—namely one Professor Arthur Jakobiak—has to know when to cut back and let others pick up the slack before he falls over dead." He placed his napkin on the table with exaggerated authority. "But he's not the only stubborn one." He wagged his finger in Claire's direction. "My great interest in your staying on here and not running off across the country has little to do with galas. My interest is in your complete recovery, in making sure you get the proper amount of time you need to convalesce. Good rest is essential to good recovery." He turned to Patrice. "Same as I've said to your father over and over again." He looked to Paul Farrow. "And, by the way, to Louis, as well. Doesn't anyone around here understand how to take care of themselves?"

Claire looked at the doctor. "I hope you know, Dr. Gomshay, that I really do appreciate your concern. Thank you." She glanced about the table, at the faces of the kind and welcoming strangers, a promise to dance with a lovely gentleman who, at the moment, was as much off his feed as she was. "I guess I have no choice. I'll do my best to stay longer and attend the gala." She looked at Patrice Jakobiak. "And please be sure to tell your father that I will look forward to dancing with him. That's very sweet." At least, she thought, this should hold them at bay. She had no intention of attending a gala. She placed her napkin on the table and stood up. "I hope you'll excuse me. It's been such a pleasure meeting all of you, but it's been kind of a long day."

Amid cheerful "good-nights" and endearing sentiment, Claire headed for the staircase with Farrow not far behind, before Dr. Gomshay called out to them.

"Sorry. Forgot altogether. Nurse Foge wanted me to ask you, Claire, if perchance you lost some kind of a fussy brass button. She gave me strict orders to inquire. Said she found it under the hospital bed."

"No, it's not mine." Claire was amused by Gomshay's apparent intimidation by his no-nonsense hospital nurse. "But please thank Nurse Foge for me."

Gomshay looked at Farrow. "How about you? Maybe even David on one of your hospital visits to our star patient here?"

Farrow shook his head. "Doesn't sound like anything David or I would wear."

Gomshay shrugged. "Well, goodnight again, Claire. Sleep well. Good rest is vital."

When Paul Farrow and Claire reached the top of the stairs, she turned to her uncle. "Thank you for the lovely evening, Paul. You have wonderful friends. I can tell. And I'm truly sorry if I embarrassed you by being so late."

"It's nothing," he said. "You can see that no one thought anything of it. They were happy to meet you, no matter what."

"I need you to know that I wasn't as reckless and inconsiderate as it must have seemed. I discovered something very important today."

"You don't have to explain."

She trained her eyes on him. "Would you mind if I do?"

"I know that *I* wouldn't mind." David was halfway up the staircase. "I've been waiting all night to find out what happened."

"Easy, David," Farrow said. "Go on, Claire. What is it you want to tell us?"

They waited.

Claire took a deep breath. "I have to admit … I really was starting to believe I might be delusional, especially hearing everyone tell me the driver is dead."

David turned his head, impatient. "He is dead."

"Yes, David, you're right," she said. "It's true. Leonard Kimmons is dead. That was confirmed today."

David raised his voice. "So, what's the problem?"

"David!" Farrow snapped.

"It's okay, Paul. Yes," she said, looking directly at David. "Leonard Kimmons is dead, but the man who drove the taxi on the night that I arrived was not Leonard Kimmons. My driver is very much alive."

The two men looked at each other.

"And," Claire went on, "whoever that man is … he is trying to kill me." She could feel the blood rushing to her head.

David raised his hand to stop her, but Farrow told her to continue.

Claire described her afternoon at the Kimmons's house, the pivotal incident with the photographs, her visit with Desiata at police headquarters, and how he allowed her to go through pages of mugshots with one of his sergeants. "I thought I had succeeded in convincing the lieutenant that my story is real and not some crazy aberration, but, frankly, I can't tell whether he's convinced or not."

"Well, it is Desiata's job to look at all of the possibilities," Farrow said. "I believe I can trust him to do that."

David leaned in. "Just remember, Claire, that your story raises all kinds of questions—reasons, motive, and so on—for which there are apparently no answers."

Claire again felt her patience waning. "Yes, Desiata and I discussed all of that. And what I believe Desiata now knows is that you're only half right, David—there are answers. We just don't have them yet."

Farrow ran his hand across his chin. "This puts everything in a whole new light. But I promise, Claire, we'll do everything we can to look after your safety, especially after last night." He looked at his watch. "It's late. The best we can do right now is to get some rest."

Claire nodded her thanks, and the three of them made their way to the bedrooms, passing the open sitting room where Parmalee was seated opposite Matthew Ettinger's wheelchair, a book in his lap.

"I'd like to go in for a minute," Claire said, "if it's okay."

Parmalee waved the three of them in.

"Hello, again, Teddy," Claire said softly, and with that, the wheelchair bolted, nearly making a full turn. Claire jumped away, now face-to-face with Matthew Ettinger, his head turned upward at an acute angle, eyes darting in frenzy.

"Whoa." Parmalee shot to his feet. "Teddy, my friend, what has come over you?"

Farrow took hold of Claire's arm, since she was clearly startled.

With a calm wave of the hand, Parmalee indicated that there was nothing to be alarmed about. "He's responding to your voice."

"Hello," Claire said again in a quiet tone.

Ettinger cocked his head as if he were blind, his right hand moving spastically on the armrest. "Vee, Vee," he called feebly, his voice flat and dronelike.

"My God!" David said.

"Well, wonder of wonders," said Parmalee.

Farrow, a grim look on his face, said nothing.

Claire looked to Parmalee for some direction.

He shrugged, "Talk to him. Tell him who you are."

Claire turned back to Ettinger. "Hello, Teddy. It's Claire," she said, her voice nearly a whisper.

"Vee?"

"I think we'd better go," Farrow said. "It's clear that he's agitated."

"Probably something in her voice," Parmalee said.

Paul Farrow gave Claire a long, probing look.

"Veeee," came the bleating voice once more.

"We might be traumatizing him in some way," Farrow said. "We ought to go."

Matthew Ettinger jerked his pale, gaunt head, then gradually, as if lulled by some command that only he could hear, retreated dull-eyed, to his customary slump, his gaze fixed, his strong hands limp. Only a sluggish blink hinted at the possibility of some distant awareness.

"Is he all right?" David had not been able to take his eyes off the scene.

"He's fine," Parmalee turned the wheelchair back around. "Never expected this, though."

"Who is Vee?" Claire asked Parmalee as he walked the three out into the hall.

The man shrugged. "Could be anybody. His first sweetheart, his fifth-grade teacher. Who can say?"

"I thought maybe his wife or daughter," Claire said.

"No, as a matter of fact, his wife's name was Robin," Parmalee said. "His daughter's name was …" He hesitated.

"Bess," said Farrow.

"Bess. That's right. I don't know why I have trouble remembering such a pretty name."

Claire had been watching her uncle. His hands were sunk deep into his pockets, his eyes tired. "Did you know them?" she asked him.

Her question seemed to take him by surprise, as if he had removed himself from the conversation and hadn't expected to be brought back into it.

"Yes," he said.

Claire waited for him to say more, but he didn't. She turned back to Parmalee. "Seems to me that whoever Vee was, she must have meant something special to him."

"Yes, but Edmund is probably right," David said. "It could be anyone, even someone he hasn't seen in thirty years. There's no way of telling."

"No, indeed," said Parmalee. "His mind, what there is of it, has become an unreasonable thing."

Claire was nearly too exhausted to sleep. After Farrow had done a final check to make sure the French doors in her room were secure before saying goodnight, she paced, sat, then paced again until finally her body could do no more. When at last she slipped under the covers, her head buzzed with the people and events of the long day behind her, but at least the day had brought its measure of relief—her sanity was most definitely intact. She had not imagined things; she was not going mad. And her gnawing visions of Matthew Ettinger made her believe all the more that sanity was surely as precious as life itself.

As she began slipping into the milky twilight, thoughts of Marjorie's dessert, and Patrice's iridescent skin, and Bob Lillian's jokes moved in a blurry whirl through her waning thoughts. Galas and foundations and gateau noisette, and one more misty recollection—Nurse Foge found a button.

Chapter Thirteen

At ten past eleven the next morning, Claire woke grudgingly, heavy-lidded, and groggy from too much sleep after too little, and tried to remember something. The room was comfortably cool and half-lit by a warm, reluctant sun. Somewhere in the woods a power saw sent an intermittent squeal amid men's voices that echoed in the denseness of the trees.

She lifted herself from the coziness of her quilt and went to the French doors. In a clearing, amid the captivating display of black green pines and autumn foliage, she could see three figures, two in hooded jackets, and one in a multi-colored vest—the one holding the saw.

Claire unlocked the doors, pulled them open, and stepped out into the brisk air. She was trying to make out who the men were, when Marjorie entered. "Oh, dear. You'll catch your death."

"Good morning, Marjorie. Who are those men. I can't tell."

Marjorie stepped out onto the terrace. "That's Bobby with the chain saw. And, let me see. Hard to tell with hooded jackets. Oh, yes, Louis. And the other is Professor Jacobiak, evidently feeling a little better today."

"Well, that's good news."

The three looked up and waved. Claire waved back as Marjorie tugged at her to come inside and closed the doors. "I've brought you up some tea and cheese toast to get you started. If you like, I'll fix you a more proper breakfast when you come down."

There was no end to the woman's kindness, Claire thought as she hugged Marjorie. "Thank you."

The deep chill had quickly motivated her toward a hot shower, and there in the steamy rush of water, it came to her as it had when she was surrendering to sleep the night before—Nurse Foge had found a button.

In a hurry to dry off, she forgot about the tenderness of her forehead and was jolted by the roughness of the towel against her bruised flesh. She pulled on her robe, picked up the telephone at the side of the bed, and dialed information to get the number of the hospital. Nurse Foge, she was told, had already gone off duty, having worked the midnight-to-eight shift. The woman at the other end was not at liberty to give out anyone's home phone number.

After identifying herself to the woman, Claire asked if Doctor Gomshay was there.

"I believe he's finishing his morning rounds," said the woman. "Let me see if he's able to come to the phone."

When Gomshay's pleasant voice came on the line, he questioned neither the interruption, for which Claire offered copious apologies, nor the fabricated explanation of her urgent interest in the button. "I had completely forgotten—it belongs to an outfit given to me by Aunt Evelyn."

Accommodating as ever, Gomshay shared the nurse's address and telephone number. "Oh, but you won't find her there till this evening," he said. "She goes right to the nursing home once a week to visit her mother."

Claire was disappointed by having to wait half a day before contacting the nurse about the button. It was a long shot, of course, but she knew that this fancy button might very well be the first tangible clue to her stalker's identity. Considering her track record for credibility, she decided to keep her notions about the button to herself, at least for the time being.

She finished getting dressed and went downstairs, where she found the rooms pleasantly deserted. She entered the kitchen and came across Marjorie in the pantry searching for something among the shelves. Bobby Tarr was standing just inside the   back door, his ears still flushed red from the cold.

"Now, stay right there," Marjorie instructed him, without looking up. "I don't want any of that pine sap from your boots on my clean floor." She reached to the back of one of the low shelves and brought out a jar whose label she closely examined. "Yes, here it is. I knew we still had a quince." She greeted Claire in her typically pleasant tone as she handed the jar to her nephew with strict instructions to deliver it at once to the professor."

"That's a very nice thought, Aunt Marge, but why don't I just take it over to the house and give it to Patrice. I don't think the professor wants to carry around a jar of quince."

"I don't know what he's doing out there anyway. He should be back in bed."

The boy took the jar. "That's what Louis said. We were out there cutting a few limbs, and, all of a sudden, the professor showed up."

"Well, hurry along now," Marjorie said, patting Bobby Tarr's arm. "Take it to Patrice, if that's what you want to do."

When the boy had gone, Marjorie invited Claire to have a seat at the kitchen table, where she set out a tray of melon, cheese, and sliced ham. "How about some eggs?"

Famished as she was, Claire gladly accepted, and was nearly finished with her morning feast as David, wearing his gym trousers, came in the back door, windblown and breathless.

"Running five miles is like running ten on a morning like this," he said. "The wind was against me all the way."

"I thought you were supposed to work this morning," Claire teased.

"And so, I did. But, then, this isn't morning any longer, is it?"

"Touche," said Claire, managing a smile. She was not happy with David, resisting her at every turn whenever she spoke about the accident and the driver as she had the night before. Still, with only a few days left of her visit, why linger over any unpleasantries. She would be as nice as she could be, then she would be gone, and with any luck at all, that would be that.

With a smug look on his face, he popped a niblet of cheese into his mouth and tossed the newspaper he'd bought onto the table. "You like the comic strips?" he asked Claire. "Who's your favorite?"

"In the Sunday paper, I like Dick Tracy and my favorite, Brenda Starr."

"What about you?" she asked him.

"Flash Gordon," he said, accepting the cup of coffee that Marjorie had poured for him.

"You need something to warm you, coming in from the cold like that," the woman said.

He grinned. "Marjorie, you are still the best ever." Then, after taking a sip of the steaming brew. "Do you know where Paul is?"

"He's been in his study all morning. He only came out once to let Louis know the saw was disturbing his work."

Claire realized she hadn't heard the saw for a while. When the master speaks, she thought.

David turned to her. "I've been a bit rough on you."

"Hmm. That's one way of putting it."

"Can I make up for it by taking you out to dinner tonight?"

Did he truly think dinner would make up for the way he continually contradicted her every word? "I think I'll just stay in, David. But thanks."

"I think a change of scenery would do you good."

"I have an errand to run this evening. Nurse Foge found a pin my aunt gave me." Claire realized she could no longer be honest with him. "I'm planning to call and stop by her apartment."

"Okay," he said. "We can do that."

The afternoon dragged. Claire spent her time in a chilly though refreshing stroll about the grounds, keeping her distance from the woods, wondering from time to time who might come to her rescue if something were to happen, since there seemed to be no one within reasonable distance most of the time. Still, while remaining alert, she enjoyed the crackle of fallen leaves underfoot and the refreshing scents of loam and cedar and evergreen. She pitched pine cones into the trees and gathered handfuls of acorns, enjoying the feel of them in her hands before giving them a toss. Pure pleasure. Oh, how she needed to feel pleasure.

Back in her room, she tried again to reach Nurse Foge, and, as she sat with the phone in her hand, she heard voices along with the slamming of car doors coming from the drive below. When there was no answer from Nurse Foge, Claire hung up and glanced out the window, catching only a glimpse of a man dressed in a white shirt and slacks getting into the driver's seat of a slate gray limousine that moved slowly down the driveway and out of sight. Claire was unable to see if anyone else was in the car.

As she came around the side of the house near the garage, she found herself face-to-face with Louis Joel. It had occurred to her before this chance meeting that she ought to find him to apologize for her behavior the day before, not that she was sorry, only that, as a guest of her uncle's, an apology seemed appropriate. Louis had done her a favor after all. Now, here she was fumbling for words, failing to hear that he, too, was offering an apology. A moment later, they were laughing, and, once again, Claire felt the glad release of tensions.

He tossed the polishing cloth he'd been using onto the bumper of the Jaguar. "I hope you don't mind my saying that you are one head-strong lady."

"I don't mind at all because it's true, which is all the more reason why I hope you don't take what I did personally. And why I hope you'll give me another chance to be friends."

"It's a deal," he said.

At ten past six, a breathless Marina Foge answered her phone, explaining that she had just walked in the door. "Of course, you can come by for the button. I'll fix us a cup of tea."

"I'm not even sure if it's the one I lost." Claire didn't like deceiving Nurse Foge, even in such a small matter, but there would be too much to explain, including the crazy possibility that this button might be linked to the man who tried to kill her in the hospital.

"It's sitting right here in front of me on the phone table," the nurse said. "Looks like brass, about the size of a dime, round like a button, but the back is missing. At first, I thought it might be a lapel pin. It has a design … initials, I think, like a monogram maybe. Oh gosh, I'm going to need to get my glasses."

"Please don't trouble yourself, Nurse Foge."

"Okay, then, I'll see you later when you get here. And please call me Marina."

Claire had somehow managed to talk David into dining at the house for one of Marjorie's offerings—light fare in the breakfast room, with its rustic brick and woody charm, where Tarr already had a fire blazing in the corner hearth, above which a rough-hewn mantle displayed a collection of gleaming, hammered copper mugs and an enormous vintage pewter tray with large ring handles. Claire was heartened to see the window wall fitted with lovely blue plaid draperies, and that they were closed to keep the night at bay or a most unwelcome watcher in the darkness beyond.

It was a casual meal, pleasant and unhurried, with some of her piano favorites coming from the handsome burl wood RCA Victor radio standing against the far wall—"If I Had You," "Till The Real Thing Comes Along." As was typical, David did most of the talking, keeping the conversation good-humored and fast paced. Farrow said little but smiled or chuckled obligingly where appropriate. At one point, he asked Claire how her day had been and apologized in a businesslike way for having been tied up.

No one brought up the Desiata mugshot incident of the day before, for which Claire was both grateful and relieved. She felt less pressured to discuss it or to recruit their support now that she held out hope for what the button might reveal and, of course, for what Desiata might be working on, all of which made it easier for her to sit quietly and just let David be David.

"We'd better get going," he said at last. "Nurse Foge will be wondering what happened to you."

Claire cringed as Farrow turned to her. "You're going to see Nurse Foge?"

"Yes." She rose from the table as she spoke. "I'm … I'm sure now that the button Dr. Gomshay asked us about is mine." She tried to avoid Paul Farrow's eyes, certain that he would instantly spot her deception. It seemed to Claire that David was as gullible as he was self-assured; Paul Farrow was as incisive as he was quiet and unassuming. Almost from the first moment she'd met her uncle in the hospital, she believed him to be a man who knew things before it was time to know them and who was not easily fooled by an untruth.

"What made you suddenly realize that?" he asked her.

"Realize what?" She looked to the doorway, praying that David would come quickly with their coats and hats.

"That the button belongs to you?" Farrow said.

"I'm not sure. I … I guess I just remembered, that's all." She was standing perfectly still now. Farrow's eyes, dark and unrelenting, had caught hers. Once again, Claire couldn't tell what she saw beyond his unsettling expression.

David returned and helped Claire into her coat. "Sure you don't want to come along?" he asked Farrow.

Claire held her breath until he declined.

"Thanks, but I may go over to the Professor's. See how he's feeling. He was out and about in the woods today, and I'm hoping he wasn't foolish enough to overdo it. He's stubborn that way. If he's up to it, we might have a game of chess."

She wondered if her uncle was really going there to see Patrice Jakobiak. Claire was intrigued by their relationship or, perhaps, the lack of it. They appeared to be such opposites, but then, that old cliché about opposites attracting was often true—Paul Farrow so solid and silent; she so flamboyant and capricious. Claire concluded with curious displeasure that Professor Jakobiak's glamorous, glossy-lipped daughter might be just the right woman for her uncle.

Farrow walked them to the front door. "So, where are you headed after Nurse Foge's?"

Claire had not even thought about it. Outside of the change in dinner plans, and the visit to the nurse's apartment, she and David had not discussed anything else.

"Just thought I'd show Claire what the amazing shoreline drive looks like at night," David said.

Farrow looked at Claire. "Sounds like it might have the makings of a date."

Looking past David's sheepish grin, Claire narrowed her eyes, not at all comfortable with the remark, but unsure why. Was it because it seemed to her that no one was remembering or believing the attempts on her life? More than once? Maybe more than twice? Or was she disturbed that Farrow would think she could be so easily agreeable to such an idea. Just how many days had she actually known David Preisler? A date? Really?

David looked at her. "Well, I suppose …"

"David offered to give me a ride to get the button." Claire's defiance was building. "His first offer was dinner, but as you know, we all had dinner here." Her jaw tightened. She turned, tugged at her new brimmed hat, and headed for the door. There was no accounting for her strong feelings toward Paul Farrow. She wanted with all her heart to dislike him intensely. What's more, David Preisler was good company when he wasn't throwing objections at Claire.

The clear night had a penetrating chill. They took David's Cord convertible, and, in a matter of minutes, with the top up, they were following the beam of their headlights down the dark, circuitous road. She was silent.

David glanced over at her more than once, seeming reticent. "He really does have a way of upsetting you, doesn't he?"

"Not really."

"He's just concerned about you."

"Hmm."

"I'm concerned about you, too, only … in a different way."

"You've all been very kind to me," she said, trying to steer away from the intimacy of David's remark. It didn't work.

"Is there anyone special in your life?" he asked.

"No one special at the moment," she said. "I prefer it that way for the time being."

"Think you'd change your mind if the right man came along?"

She didn't respond.

"Your Aunt Evelyn never married, did she? Neither has your uncle. Must run in the family." He tried to make light of it with a chuckle, but she wasn't amused.

"You're forgetting about my mother. She was, after all, their sister. Besides, from the looks of it, Patrice Jakobiak might be out to change my uncle's marital status." She looked at him. "Isn't that so?"

"I don't know. They see each other, but not much differently than you saw them at the dinner table. Of course, Professor Jakobiak would like nothing better than to see them together. He loves Paul, and not just because of Paul's great generosity to Arthur's foundation. As for Patrice, there's no telling what Paul Farrow's true feelings are. He's always played things close to the vest."

"Do you like him?" she asked.

He hesitated before answering. "Yes. On the whole. I admire him. But he keeps me on the outside too."

This surprised Claire. "I thought you two were quite close."

"You have to remember—first and foremost, we're business associates. I work for your uncle. Don't let the fact that we work in an intimate atmosphere fool you. Most of what we talk about is business. A lot of your uncle's time is spent alone in his private study."

"Doing what?"

"Working on his latest designs, writing his book. He's been working on that for some time."

"That's interesting. What kind of a book?"

"Architecture. Lucy does the typing for him, when she can."

"I thought she works for you."

"She does, but remember, I'm Paul's associate."

"Does she like working with him?"

"Not sure. But I don't have to tell you that Paul Farrow can be an intimidating figure. He's a bit of a perfectionist, and I guess that might scare people off, although, honestly, everybody likes your uncle." He shrugged. "And Lucy hasn't complained yet." He laughed. "Well, not too much, anyway."

"Yes," she said, more curious than ever. "Who knows?"

And couldn't she relate to that? As exasperating as Paul Farrow has been, he'll completely upset her dislike of him, she thought, with some unexpected kindness or sentiment. Claire wasn't even sure that she wouldn't miss him.

"I'm curious, David. You talk about Paul and his sister, Evelyn, not being married, but what about you?"

It surprised her that he didn't answer at first—he was always the more voluble one in the group. Why hold back now?

"I've dated."

"Anyone special?"

"Once. A long time ago. We were engaged, actually."

"Oh, I'm sorry. I hope I haven't overstepped."

"You haven't. I don't talk about it much because it was a painful lesson—I allowed my work schedule to dominate my life."

Her question had brought him back to an unhappy time in his life, and she was sorry about it. But he had also hit a sympathetic cord in her. He was more vulnerable than she would have guessed. They said very little after that.

Chapter Fourteen

At a little before eight, they arrived at the neat five-story apartment complex on Westphal Street. With a deftness otherwise reserved for brain surgeons, David maneuvered the Cord into a space along the curb that appeared to Claire too small to park a baby carriage. He then insisted on going with her despite the well-illuminated and welcoming appearance of the place. There were three buildings forming a triptych beyond a large landscaped court that afforded entry through a tall stone arch with the words Westphal Arms scrolled in wrought iron across the top.

In the vestibule of the building on the left, David pressed the small black button labeled "3-E FOGE." Almost immediately, a shrill buzzer signaled their admittance through the heavy double glass doors into the lobby, where there were two slow elevators. Marina Foge's apartment was the second door to the right along a well-appointed, warmly lit corridor. Claire rang the bell and waited, then rang again, but other than the chime of the bell on the other side of the door, all was quiet.

The elevator door opened, and a preoccupied man of about sixty, dressed in tan coveralls and carrying a small curved section of black hose, exited. Fastened to his belt was a ring of keys that jingled in rhythm with his gait. Claire and David recognized at once that he must be the building custodian. The man eyed them as he passed without altering his pace or the intent expression on his face. By the time they had rung again, the man was past them. He turned and paused with apparent curiosity as to why they were not being given entry, and started back.

"She buzzed us in a few minutes ago." David shrugged. "But now there's no answer."

"Did you hear the bell on the inside?" the man asked. "Maybe it isn't working."

"Yes," Claire said. "We heard it."

David walked toward the man. "Maybe you can help us?"

Claire called again. "Nurse Foge, it's Claire Fournaris." This time she knocked, and the door gave. With the door now slightly ajar, she called again, fearful of intruding. "Nurse Foge? Hi. It's Claire."

As the opening widened, she saw that there were lights on in the apartment and ducked her head in. "Hi. Nurse Foge. It's Claire Fournaris." The neat setting was a stylish contemporary mix of muted sage and ecru with the gleam of glass and stainless steel. A pang of anxiety gripped her as she dipped her head farther in and scanned the room, continuing to call out. The telephone lay strewn on the floor, and there, next to the glass-topped coffee table, lay Nurse Marina Foge, her head angled sideways, her eyes open in a fixed gaze.

David pressed behind Claire in the door way. "My God."

"Get an ambulance!" Claire blurted out. Heart pounding, she stepped cautiously toward the woman and heard a groan. She moved to her side with no idea how to help without causing further injury. "Help is coming, Marina. Someone will be here soon."

The door flew open as David rushed back in.

The woman's mouth moved in a raspy groan. Claire leaned closer.

"It's okay. Marina. Help is coming." Claire prayed this was true and that it would not be too late. "Help will be here soon."

The custodian was in the room now. "Good Lord, what happened here?"

"We don't dare try to move her," David said. "I've already called for an ambulance and the police from a neighbor's. They're on their way."

Claire signaled them to be quiet. "She's trying to say something." She saw the slightest flicker in the woman's eyes. "What is it, Marina?"

A siren's shrill peal grew louder in the night. Claire felt pressure on her wrist and looked down to see that Marina was clasping the cuff of Claire's blouse. There was a long hoarse sound, like a rush of air through a hollow tube as the woman tried to speak. Claire stroked Marina's hand. "You're going to be fine," Claire said, not believing her own words.

Marina's face stiffened into a desperate plea.

"What is it, Marina? Oh, God. I wish I knew how to help you." Claire felt a pop at her wrist.

With a feeble burst of energy, the woman pulled the button from Claire's cuff, uttering something nearly inaudible.

As David covered the woman with a blanket from the bedroom, Claire looked up. "I can't make out what she's saying." She leaned down with her ear close to Marina's mouth. "Say it again, Marina. Please."

Except for her erratic breathing, Nurse Foge lay silent.

"Marina," said David, "are you trying to tell us something about what happened to you?"

The woman's eyes fluttered.

"Was there something … someone?"

Marina's dazed brown eyes fluttered rapidly. She gasped.

"Was someone here?" Claire pressed.

David drew closer. "Did someone do this to you, Marina?"

Claire felt the woman's hand jerk. She looked down to see Marina Foge's right hand lying open. The white fabric-covered button from Claire's blouse sat squarely in the center of Marina's palm.

Claire stared momentarily at the button, then at the woman's colorless face, puzzled by what appeared to be such a bizarre action. Then, like a seven-letter crossword answer that jolts you awake at two in the morning, it hit Claire. "My God. David. The button!" Claire gently picked up Marina Foge's hand and clasped it in hers. "That's it, Marina, isn't it? Someone came for the button. The one I was coming to get."

Marina Foge's eyes rolled upward, her face thick and ghostly, as Claire leaned over her, rocking.

"I don't follow," David said.

"Marina, please hold on. Please. Can you tell me who it was. Who did this to you? Who came for the button?"

A commotion in the hallway brought frenzied voices and footsteps. Five medics rushed Claire and David to one side so they could work.

"She's saying something." The young medic leaned closer. "Sounds like …

H. A."

Marine Foge's eyes suddenly widened.

"She said it again—H. A," The medic repeated as he tended to her injury.

The woman breathed a dry, harsh utterance from lips barely able to move.

All Claire could see was the heightened desperation in the Marina Foge's face, a look of anguish that registered in Claire like the chill of death itself. The final sound of life a mournful bleating, one disconsonant chord that trailed off into eternal silence.

"We've lost her," said the medic. He looked at his watch. "7:48 p.m."

David took Claire by the arm and led her out to the hall where they leaned against the wall in stunned silence.

"I can't believe it," Claire whispered. "I just can't. Such a beautiful, kind woman." She covered her face with her hands.

"Well, this is a first for me." David ran his fingers through his hair. "I never saw anything like this before."

For a few minutes longer, they stayed in the hallway, half-watching the medics finish yet another task that was likely quite familiar to them. Then, David looked directly at Claire. "What was all that business about the button? And why do I get the feeling you haven't been honest with me … again?"

"It's … it's hard to be honest with you," Claire said, after a long pause. "If I had told you the truth about the button, would you have let us stop by here? The answer is no. So, no, I couldn't be truthful with you … again." They made their way along the corridor, a short distance from Marina's apartment, knowing the police would have questions for them.

"So, just what is the truth?" he said.

"The button belongs to the man who's trying to kill me. I'm sure of it now. I wanted to get hold of it to see if there was some way it could help identify him."

"You're right. I wouldn't have bought it. I wouldn't have wanted to bring you here."

"Do you buy it now?" Claire said, a cynical tone in her voice. "Now that there's been a murder? Another murder? Is that convincing enough for you, David?"

David put his hand up. "Hey, wait. Let's slow down here. Just because you thought you knew something about some button that Marina Foge had, I don't think it's wise to connect that with something she was struggling to tell you. We couldn't even understand what she was trying to say. So, you just can't sum it all up as murder. The poor woman fell and hit her head. Not everything terrible that happens is about murder."

As Claire glanced at David in disbelief, she noticed a round-faced officer coming toward them, a notepad in his hand.

"I understand you found the body," he said in a deep voice. The nametag on the lapel pocket of his police uniform said "Wolrath."

Claire nodded.

"I'm sorry," he said. "I can imagine how hard this must be, but I do need to ask a few questions."

"Can't this wait?" David said.

"It's all right, Officer," Claire said, turning her shoulder to David.

"You were acquainted with the victim?" Wolrath asked.

The word *victim* added fresh realization to the horror of the moment. "Yes, I knew her."

"You can make positive identification, then?"

"Yes. Her name is Marina Foge. She's … she *was* … a nurse at the hospital. With the officer jotting notes, Claire recounted the details of her horrifying discovery and of the moments that followed. As she spoke, numb and unanimated, she found it difficult to believe her own words.

"You say the person you think did this also tried to kill you?" Wolrath asked.

"Yes."

"And have you reported this to the police?"

"Yes, she has, Sergeant," said a voice from behind.

Even before turning, Claire recognized the flat, sure tone of Lieutenant Desiata. Thank God, she thought. Thank God.

"Evening, Lieutenant," Wolrath said. "Have you been briefed?"

"Some. On the way up. What have you got?"

"Miss Fournaris, here, found the body and was able to speak with the victim before she passed. Miss Fournaris believes this may not be an accident."

"I'm not surprised," said Desiata, his eyes trained impassively on Claire. "And how did both of you just happen to be here at such a critical moment?"

"We didn't just happen to be here, Lieutenant," Claire said as, one by one, a small, grim gathering of residents grew at a distance along the corridor. "Nurse Foge knew I was coming to pick up a button that she had found under my hospital bed. I believe that button belonged to the man who tried to smother me that night in the hospital."

Desiata took Wolrath's pad and glanced over the notes. Then, as he entered the apartment, he instructed the Sergeant to have Claire and David wait for him in the kitchen. "And please don't touch anything," he added, looking directly at Claire.

"May I use the telephone?" David asked. "I'd like to let Paul Farrow know what's happened."

"No." Desiata motioned them toward the kitchen.

The twenty minutes they sat waiting felt like hours. The sergeant stood to one side, occasionally rocking on his feet, while opposite them a plainclothesman probed the corners and countertops, making notes as he went. Claire looked about the spacious rectangle full of the comfortable clutter of opened mail, hanging spoons, quilted potholders, and fringed tea towels sporting embroidered ducks. A singed oven mitt was set to one side of the stovetop, while the hand that last used it lay lifeless in the next room. All the time, the initials H. A. throbbed in Claire's head.

"Do you have any ideas about H. A.?" It was the first question Desiata asked when he finally came into the kitchen.

Claire shook her head.

Desiata looked at David. "Logic tells me it's something you might be more apt to recognize, Mr. Preisler, since you're from around here—a person's name, a place, anything familiar?"

"Not a thing, Lieutenant. I've been going over it in my head. And, by the way, how does a homicide detective end up at a routine trip-and-fall death?"

"I happened to hear the name Fournaris."

At Desiata's request, Claire explained in detail the circumstances surrounding the object she believed to be a button.

"And you say that Marina Foge had this button in her possession?"

"Yes. When I spoke with her earlier, she told me it was there in front of her on the telephone table, but she couldn't make out what was on it because she didn't have her glasses."

Desiata turned to Sergeant Wolrath. "Anything turn up that looks like a loose button or something like it?"

"Not yet, Sir. But there is a pair of women's eyeglasses on the floor next to the telephone."

"Which means," Claire said, "that she had gotten her glasses and was trying to tell me what the initials were."

Desiata looked over the pages on his notepad. "Is my understanding correct, Sergeant, that the apartment was not ransacked?"

"That's right, Sir. It doesn't look as if anything is out of place."

"Then, doesn't it fit?" Claire said. "The murderer came for one thing—the button. When he got it, he had to kill her. Maybe he was even someone she knew personally." Claire put her hand to her lip, thoughtful, then got to her feet, wide-eyed. "Lieutenant, the murderer must have been right here with her when we arrived. She buzzed us in downstairs only minutes before we found her." She turned to David, animated now. "Don't you remember how quickly the buzzer sounded after we rang. She probably already knew she was in danger and saw a chance for help. She jumped for the buzzer, and the killer hit her."

Desiata turned to Wolrath. "Make sure you dust that buzzer for prints."

One of the uniformed investigators entered the kitchen with a small white envelope. "Lieutenant, we found this under the body."

Desiata looked inside the envelope without touching the contents, then he looked at Claire. "Miss Fournaris, can you identify this as the button you were looking for?"

Claire's excitement vanished when what she saw was a plain tan button with two tiny holes used for threading. "I don't understand. That's just an ordinary button, not the one I'm talking about."

"Miss Fournaris, was there anything special you noticed about the body, besides the head wound?"

Claire paused, her eyes roaming the room, gathering her thoughts. "Nurse Foge was slightly turned to one side."

"Anything else?"

"I … don't know. I had never seen someone in that situation. I never had someone die right in front of me."

"Did you happen to notice," he said as he folded the envelope and handed it back to the investigator, "the telephone cord wrapped loosely around the victim's ankle?"

The phone cord? No, she hadn't seen that. How did she miss it, and where was Lieutenant Desiata going with this? "I can't say that I did. It was all so …"

"And what might that suggest to you, Miss Fournaris?"

Now, she knew where he was going with this. She glanced at David standing by, tight-lipped. He knew, as well. "I don't know what to make of it," she said.

David took a step forward. "Maybe I can offer something, Lieutenant."

Desiata folded his arms and leaned back against the counter. "I'd like to hear it."

"Nurse Foge rang the buzzer. But then, when she turned to cross the room, she caught her foot in the telephone cord, stumbled to the floor, bringing the phone with her. Isn't that the obvious likelihood, Lieutenant? That Nurse Foge died from hitting her head when she fell?"

The Lieutenant had kept his eyes on Claire. "Let's ask Miss Fournaris."

Claire was seething. David. Again. Going against her word. No support. No confidence. "I think I've probably said enough, Lieutenant. Make of this what you will. May I go now?"

The drive home with David at the wheel seemed endless. She had nothing more to say to him. Not tonight. Not ever. She would be gone in a few days and good riddance.

In a dark corner of the top-floor stairwell, the shadowy figure clutched a button, knowing the police would not search. Who would believe another hysterical account from a delusional woman? All of this about a silly button, they would surmise. There was a button, after all, but isn't it clear that it came from the victim's trench coat tossed over the back of a nearby chair? The nurse had just returned home. A button had come off her coat. Murder? Hardly. It was merely a most accommodating phone cord. Now, just go home, lovely Claire. We'll be meeting soon again.

Chapter Fifteen

Lieutenant Desiata had given Claire and David instructions before allowing them to leave Marina Foge's apartment. He would be in touch soon. In the meantime, they could tell of their visit to the nurse's home but not the real reason for going. They could say that she was still alive when they arrived but not that she'd said anything. They would not mention the button. And they would not speak of murder. None of it, except to Paul Farrow.

It was a little before eleven when they pushed in through the front door on a frigid gust. After Tarr took their coats and hats, David led the way to the study, where they found Paul Farrow reading in a corner by the fire.

"Chilly out there tonight," Farrow said.

David went to the small table and poured a glass of sherry for himself and Claire. "For you?" he asked, gesturing to Farrow.

"No thanks."

"How's Arthur doing?" David asked.

"He's okay. Just not recovering very well from whatever is ailing him. No sooner had I gotten there that he nearly passed out. Patrice took him up to bed, so I came home. Just as well— I've been too distracted to be a good chess partner. What about you? A good drive along the shoreline?" He looked at Claire, then got to his feet. "Hey, you're shaking like a leaf. What's going on?" He led her to a chair by the fire. "Has something happened?"

She took a sip of the sherry but said nothing.

"Something happened, all right," David said. "Marina Foge is dead. We're not sure how. She tripped … hit her head … or something."

"What do you mean 'or something.'"

"Claire found the woman, gravely injured. She thinks it was murder. Desiata was there. I'm not sure what he thinks. We are not to speak of this to anyone, except you." David went on to explain the details that, for the sake of Claire's safety, only Paul Farrow was permitted to hear.

"Good Lord!" Farrow stood in front of Claire. "Why didn't you let us know what was going on? When Gomshay asked you about the button that Nurse Foge had found, you and I both said it wasn't ours. Then, you go off on this crazy errand?" He turned to David. "And you go right along with her? You have to know by now what could have happened. For a killer, one more victim doesn't matter." He ran his hand across the top of his head. "Claire—" he said, his voice dropping off.

"At first, I didn't know about the button," she said, her voice low, her tired gaze settled on her sherry glass. "It didn't register till … I don't know … later on. David had no idea what was going on. I told him that Nurse Foge had found a pin my aunt had given me."

She could see that Farrow was frustrated with her. Yet, somewhere in what he had said was a note of tenderness that she hadn't heard before. She hardly cared at this point as realization set in—a gruesome experience, another betrayal from David, Desiata and his noncommittal ways. She looked up at her uncle, the emotional turbulence grinding inside her. She was not prepared for any of this. "I'm very tired," she said, setting the glass on the table. "I'd better go up."

Paul Farrow took her hand to help her from the chair, and turned to David. "Regardless of what Desiata may think at the moment, we can't take a chance on Claire's safety. It very well may turn out that she's been right all along."

She left the room, saying nothing at all, and made her way up the stairs to her room. Mindless exhaustion had set in, and at nearly one-thirty in the morning, it still had not released her to sleep. Even the welcome glass of sherry she had sipped in dazed silence hadn't helped. She kept going over everything that had happened—the quick buzzer, the cuff button, the crazy notion that what happened to poor Marina Foge was an accident.

She would go over these again and again like a mantra. And there would be no forgetting the look of desperate helplessness on the nurse's face, or her last cry of life, the bleating, disconsonant H. A. There was something else about Marina Foge in that last moment of her life. Claire couldn't put her finger on it. More than anguish; a kind of startled protest, as if in a brief, final pinch of clarity, she had discovered the amazing fact of her own imminent death. Is that all it was? She went through the list of the only people she knew here including Paul Farrow's friends. Who or what was H. A.?

At about three, she decided to go down to the kitchen for a glass of warm milk to help her sleep. As she passed the second-floor sitting room, she noticed, as she had earlier on the way to her room, that neither Edmund Parmalee nor Matthew Ettinger were there. She found Parmalee in the kitchen having a cup of tea. He smiled his strong, solid smile. "No sleep again?"

All she had for him was the thinnest of greetings as she joined him at the table. "It seems that sleep comes only when it's good and ready."

"Have some Chamomile," he said, getting up from the table. He brought back another cup and saucer from the cabinet and set them before her. From the lightness of his mood, Claire assumed he had not yet heard about Marina Foge.

"How is Mr. Ettinger tonight?"

"He's having a little trouble adjusting," said Parmalee. "But he'll be fine."

"Adjusting?"

"New surroundings. New voices. The feel of a place, the sound. He notices changes, as you saw for yourself."

"I don't understand," Claire said.

"Forgive me. I just assumed you knew. We admitted Matthew to a special care facility today."

Claire remembered the dark gray limousine in the drive earlier in the day and the driver dressed in white. "No, I didn't know. I'm sorry to hear that."

"They sent a car for him with an attendant. Of course, your uncle and I accompanied him."

"But why so suddenly. Is he ill—I mean, worse?"

Parmalee shook his head. "Your uncle's idea. He feels there's been a lot of activity in the house lately and that Matthew would benefit from more restful surroundings. Of course, Matt was due for a complete work-up next month anyway. So, all this means is that he's going in a bit earlier."

"Then, this is just a temporary situation?"

Parmalee filled Claire's cup from the porcelain teapot. "We expect him back in a week or so."

Claire presumed that Parmalee meant Matthew would be back as soon as she was gone and things returned to normal at the Farrow estate. She didn't resent the decision. It was obvious that Matthew Ettinger had experienced a fair amount of agitation in her presence. It seemed a kind gesture on the part of her uncle to be so considerate of his friend's condition.

"What will you do in the meantime? Claire asked.

"Oh, I'll be here. Your uncle has asked me to … well … take on, let's say, security duties. That's why I'm here at this odd hour. Just being attentive, you might say."

"My apologies," Claire said, adding a bit of milk to her tea. "I seem to be interfering with everyone's life."

"Not at all. We're quite a bit like family around here and that means doing what needs to be done for each other." He reached over and tapped her teacup with his.

She acknowledged the sweetness of his gesture with a dip of her head. "How long have you been working for my uncle?"

"He hired me before he even closed on the estate. Long distance. He wanted to be sure Matthew would have good care from the moment they moved in."

"I believe I detect a slight accent," she said.

"I forget that I have one since I no longer hear it." He laughed. "I was born in the East Indies—Indonesia, to be specific. My father was English, a doctor. My mother South African."

"How interesting. You're the first person I've ever met from that part of the world."

"Then, I can only hope I represent my homeland well."

"Very well." He was easy to talk with, Claire thought. She liked his manners. "It doesn't look as if you have much time to yourself. Do you have a family, if you don't mind my asking?"

"My wife … Juliet. That was her name. She died of polio about ten years ago."

"Oh, I'm sorry, Edmund. So sorry."

"We had no children. So, you can see that mine is the perfect profession for someone going through life on his own, you might say." He took a sip of tea.

"Well, it's clear that you not only do important work, but you are well respected by everyone here, including my uncle's friends. Hannah Lillian made a comment about you just the other night. She said there was definitely a bit of a void when you were away recently.

"Well, thank you for saying that, Miss Fournaris."

"Please call me Claire."

"And, yes, Claire, I do have a full schedule, but there are a few games of tennis once or twice during the week with your uncle. We've got a pretty able foursome when David and Louis Joel join in. You've seen the tennis courts, I presume."

"Yes, David showed me the other day. I've played a little but not very well."

They laughed.

She looked down into her cup. "You know, now that my aunt is gone, I think I'll be able to relate to that sense you had about going through life on your own." She set her cup down. "But I'm trying to remain optimistic about one day having a family of my own."

When they had said goodnight, Claire made her way to the study at the end of the living room to read for a while, hoping to convert her nervous exhaustion into sleepiness. The house had an agreeable quietness, a certain tranquility that enabled her to feel more relaxed. Despite everything, and lacking a rational explanation for it, she felt safe there.

When she opened the study doors, she was relieved to find that a lamp had been left on; she wouldn't have to grope in the darkness for a switch. The room was empty, the hearth still flickering with a comforting glow. She paused, feeling pleased by the room's hospitable ambience and the sweet lingering woodiness of pipe tobacco that allowed her a deep, contented breath.

As she closed the doors behind her, she was surprised to see one of the doors to her uncle's private study at the far end standing ajar. In the light from a single desk lamp, she glimpsed what appeared to be a spread of drawings. She approached with cautious steps, unable to ignore the notion that she was trespassing, yet unwilling to resist the invitation of the room's entry. She almost held her breath as she pushed the door wider.

"I sometimes hesitate to go in myself."

The sound of Paul Farrow's voice from behind gave Claire a jolt that caused her to spin around, nearly losing her balance. He'd been stretched out on the sofa, a book in one hand, his hair slightly mussed. She had been unable to see him lying there reading.

"I … I didn't know anyone was here." She could feel her face hot with the flush of embarrassment. "I came in to read for a while. I saw the door open. It seemed odd." She realized that the words were pouring out of her mouth in an effort to explain away her snooping. "I guess I became curious. I'm sorry." She moved to leave.

"I take it you couldn't sleep either." He got to his feet.

She shrugged. "I just left Mr. Parmalee in the kitchen. He fixed me tea."

"I shouldn't have been so sharp with you earlier." His voice was mellow, his tone so conciliatory that she forgave him at once and couldn't help noticing that a pattern was developing—what was it about him that, on the one hand, he could so easily anger or intimidate her, yet, on the other, could cause her unhesitatingly to put all bad feeling toward him aside. Evelyn might have said it was his sincerity? A certain boyish brooding that sometimes made him seem unreasonable yet vulnerable. Maybe, he was, after all, just a very ordinary man with a simplicity of heart that proved too fragile for whatever complexities occupied his life. Maybe that included his relationship with Patrice Jakobiak. Claire had taken notice that when the Professor was too ill to enjoy a game of chess, her uncle hadn't lingered for a visit with Jakobiak's lovely daughter.

"You had every right to be sharp with me. I should have realized I might be endangering myself, as well as David. I ought to have confided in him … and you."

She put her hand up. "Please, don't get up on my account."

"It's okay. I've had my fill of the sea for another night."

She gave him a quizzical look, and he gestured to the table where he'd placed the book. "Ocean liners. I like to read about them. How they're built. Have you ever sailed?"

"Once. With Aunt Evelyn. You remember—we took the Queen Mary to Europe. I think it was 1935 or '36. I loved it. How about you?"

He leaned against the arm of the sofa. "I—"

Claire interrupted. "Oh, my goodness … I'm forgetting. Of course, you have."

He gave her a blank look.

"Your Navy days. I'm surprised that didn't satisfy any longing you ever had for open water."

There was an awkward silence. "Yes … well … that was a long time ago, and I think you'd agree that Navy boats are a far cry from the Queen Mary."

"I can see that must be true." She sensed his discomfort talking about himself and changed the subject. "Mr. Parmalee told me about Matthew going to a facility. It was the first I'd heard. I'm sorry about it."

"I thought it best for him. I'm sure Edmund explained that it's just routine. He's due for a thorough physical."

"Actually." She put her finger to her lip. "I understand that he wasn't really due for another month or so."

"And?"

"And I feel he's had to go because of me. Because of this grand disturbance I've managed to create since coming here."

"There's no harm done. And certainly none of what's been going on has been any of your creation. Go easy on yourself."

There was another silence. She wondered whether to stay or go. She decided to linger. "David was telling me you're working on a book on architecture. I admit I was curious when I thought I could see drawings on your desk just now."

"There's a lot involved—especially research. But it's coming along, little by little. David helps a lot with other business, as you've seen. And Lucy's an awfully patient helper. Smarter and much more resilient than her gentle ways might suggest. It can get a little crazy around here at times, and she is definitely fit for this environment." He looked at the mantle clock. "Nearly four. At least one of us had better go up and do the best we can to get some rest."

Claire chuckled at the lightness of his tone. How strange he is, she thought—elegant and handsome, even when disheveled, capable of great sensitivity, yet usually distant. Willing to give so much of himself or nothing at all.

Normandy startled her by coming from nowhere and brushing her ankle, then he turned and brushed it again. Claire reached down to stroke his back.

"His opportunities for new friendships are rare," Farrow said. "This one seems to have worked out well; he likes you." He gestured over his shoulder to the corner bookcases by the French doors. "By the way, there's some good poetry on those shelves. It may help take your mind off things. Hopkins and Frost sometimes work best for me—simple, beautiful, and uncomplicated." He lightly jabbed a finger in the direction of the bookcases. "But stay away from Dickinson."

"She's beautifully morbid, isn't she?"

"Indeed," Farrow said, "'Because I could not stop for death, he kindly stopped for me.'"

His quoting poetry surprised her.

"Would you like me to add a log to the fire?"

"No. Thanks," she said, as one still taken by the unexpected. "I'll be heading up soon myself."

As Farrow headed for the door, Normandy sauntered to his side, then darted ahead of him, playful.

"It's hard to believe you ever hated cats," she said with a smile.

Farrow raised his arm and said goodnight.

"Wait," she said, nodding in the direction of his private study, "you didn't lock the doors."

"I know," he said, in a playful whisper, and left the room.

If she had to, she could not define him. Nor could she explain her perpetual effort to try. She couldn't help comparing him with other men she had known—Steven, with his selfish concern for his mastery of handball. He cancelled dates if a match came up. He often teased her about reading too much. It didn't last. Neither did her relationship with Gordon. Such a good man but so timid about life—afraid to go horseback riding, afraid to try skiing. After breaking up with him, she tried both. Oh, how she might have enjoyed a man who loved poetry. Ahh, well.

She closed the door to his private study and turned to leave. It occurred to her with some surprise that neither one of them had mentioned Marina Foge. Yet, it seemed obvious that since neither of them could sleep, both had been deeply affected by the nurse's death. There is a kind of bond formed, she thought, when two people can share a common problem or unpleasantness, tragedy even, without the need to speak of it. Claire wondered if that's what had just taken place. She couldn't be sure, but she liked the idea and found it hopeful.

Chapter Sixteen

On Monday morning, surprised by a rare restful night, Claire dressed for her trip into Manhattan. Finally, to get this done and move on from the madness of this past week. Downstairs, on her way to the kitchen, she met Lucy Conant scurrying with an armful of files toward David's office in the east study. "Nice to see you, Lucy." What must all these friends of her uncle's think of her? She almost wished they knew what she'd been going through.

"Hi. Don't mind me, Claire. Busy day. There are a few things I want to get out of the way before you and David leave for the city.

"Sorry for having to take David away."

"Not at all. Many days look like this even when David's not going anywhere."

"I know about days like this at the college. I guess we all have them."

In the kitchen, Claire was surprised to find Patrice Jakobiak and Hannah Lillian having breakfast. "What a nice surprise!"

"Good morning to you," said Hannah. "Marjorie offered us the breakfast room, but why fuss. Kitchen's best; don't you think? And we only came by to pick up your uncle's check. Fundraiser stuff. But I guess by now you know Marjorie."

"Yes, I do." Claire liked Hannah Lillian from that first night she'd met her—down-to-earth, easy to talk with. She still wasn't sure about Patrice. "Kitchens are the best, although Marjorie's cooking would taste good even on the floor of the garage," Claire said.

There was laughter, but from Patrice, only what appeared to be a forced smile.

"Well, I guess even I have to agree with that," said Patrice, before taking a sip of coffee.

It occurred to Claire that when Patrice Jakobiak was not playing the role of flirtatious nymph in the company of Paul Farrow, she was somber and aloof, which Claire didn't consider very alluring qualities. "How is the professor? My uncle says he's been up and down with not much lasting improvement. I'm sorry to hear that."

"Thank you for asking. Honestly, no one can figure it out. He's on the mend one minute and back in bed the next. It seems to have started with whatever Louis had."

"Hard to figure," Claire said.

Hannah dabbed her lip with the corner of her napkin. "Now, remember, Claire—we're all planning on seeing you next weekend at the gala."

"I'm looking forward to it, Hannah." She sat and poured herself a cup of coffee, then took one of the breakfast scones that Marjorie had set out. "Patrice, please be sure to tell your father I'm holding him to that dance he promised." Claire sincerely hoped she would be gone by then.

"He'll be happy that you said that. Thank you. That may be the thing that gets him moving again."

Hannah gave Claire a gleeful look. "Wear something that shimmers. Although you'll dazzle no matter what you wear."

"May I be terribly candid?" said Patrice. "If it weren't for the fact that you are Paul Farrow's niece, it would bother the heck out of me that the two of you are under the same roof."

Claire felt her face flush. "Tell me. What is he like, my uncle? Both of you know him far better than I do."

"Kind," said Hannah. "Honorable."

Patrice looked directly at Claire. "Distant, as you may have discovered."

"Yes, I would have to agree," said Hannah. "My husband says Paul Farrow circles and circles but doesn't land very often. Still, a very good man, though. He drew up the plans for Bob's new dental office, no charge. He's quite generous. And he never wants any public thanks or praise."

Patrice lifted her chin. "It's only because of Paul Farrow that my father's treasured enterprise of searching out rare artifacts from around the world is flourishing. And he's having the time of his life, doing it—going on digs in places like Egypt and Turkey."

"I think he's been on two this year," Hannah said. "Bob had planned to go with him, but he had to be somewhere else." She took a sip of coffee. "But getting back to your uncle, he also gave Roland and Marjorie a new car for Christmas, and—" The wall clock caught her eye. "Oh, dear, we've got to get a move on."

They exited the kitchen just as Marjorie made her way along the corridor. Claire said goodbye and returned to the kitchen, where she cleared the table and cleaned the breakfast plates. When Marjorie came in, Claire could see that the woman appeared a bit disturbed. After thanking Claire for tidying up, she began to firmly pluck leaves from an overgrown fern that normally sat on the mahogany side table in the entry. A jar of quince was set on the counter beside it.

"Oh, you are a busy lady, Marjorie. You've even made more quince."

"Not more." The woman seemed to attack one of the twigs with her snippers. "It's the very same jar I gave Bobby to take to the Professor's daughter."

"Oh, so, it didn't make it to its destination."

Marjorie winced. "Seems like a small thing, doesn't it? And it would be if it wasn't happening more and more." She turned the potted plant and snipped at another straggly vine with her shears. "And more."

"Sorry to hear that. It must be very frustrating."

"He was always a good boy. His mother was Rollie's sister. We never met the father. He left before Bobby was born. Rollie is the closest thing to a father that the boy has ever known." She continued working on the plant. "Beatrice. That was his mother. She did a good job raising her son, but he was so timid and lonely. It could break your heart." She sighed and shook her head. "Then, a little over two years ago, Beatrice got sick. Bobby quit school to help her. He wouldn't listen to anyone who offered to help so he could stay in school. He had two or three jobs at a time. We tried talking with him, but no use. We sent money to help pay for the doctors. They told him the worst, and he figured the more money he had, the more the doctors would be able to keep her alive, until it reached the point where …" She stopped and looked directly at Claire. "He started stealing."

"Oh. I'm so sorry, Marjorie."

"Yes. Well, it was just little things at first. A bit of money from a man's pocket or a woman's purse. He even stole from us when we visited Beatrice in the hospital. And he went right on stealing, mostly from people he knew. It's not that anyone made light of it. They knew there was a problem. Still, they took pity on him. Rollie had long talks with him, and the boy would make promises that he never kept."

The kitchen door swung open, and David came in. "Oh, here you are," he said, looking at Claire.

Marjorie picked up the white fluted pot. "I think this one's ready to go back," she said, faking a bright tone.

"Please, wait." Claire gestured for Marjorie to stay. "David, would you mind please giving us a few minutes?"

David looked at the two of them. "Oh. Sorry," he said with an embarrassed smirk. "I just want to let you know that Desiata is here. We're also going to have to leave pretty soon for the city." He gave a quick nod. "We'll be in the study. Sorry, again."

Claire felt her heart sink when she heard that Desiata had arrived. She was anxious about what he'd have to say, what he might or might not have come up with. But, for the moment, that was another story. "Please finish what you were saying, Marjorie. About when Beatrice died. Did the stealing stop?"

Marjorie set the pot on the counter. "The stealing got worse. Expensive jewelry. A neighbor's car. We tried to get him to come live with us, but he refused. There was nothing we could do. The boy was eighteen."

"I hope you and Rollie don't blame yourselves in any way."

"We tried counseling, but he just wasn't ready. We were told he had all this anger inside and feelings he couldn't handle. Rollie was beside himself."

"What about now? He's here. He seems helpful, even though he gets sidetracked."

"That Iowa neighbor pressed charges over the car. He apologized to Rollie but that didn't save Bobby from facing a judge. We finally confided in Mr. Farrow, and he flew out with us to Iowa along with his lawyer. They managed to get the boy probation in exchange for a promise that he would come to live here with us and go for therapy."

"Did he go along with it? Keep his promise?"

"Oh, that first taste of a jail cell changed everything. He was scared to death. Told all of us how grateful he was. And ..." She made a sweeping motion with her hand. "You can see that this is the perfect place for a young man. So many good role models for him—your uncle and Paul and Louis, Edmund Parmalee, so kind and generous with their time. The professor. Hannah Lillian's husband, Bob."

"Don't forget your own husband."

"Thank God for Rollie." Marjorie pressed her eyes shut. "Anyway, he saw a psychologist twice a week up until just about a month or so ago. He knows that if he slips, he's going back to jail."

"And you're worried? You think he might slip?"

"Well, it's odd, and please, don't be offended." She touched Claire's arm. "But he seemed to be doing okay until just about the time you arrived. He's been nervous. We feel he's holding back, hiding something. When I saw you both talking, I was afraid something might have happened between you."

"That wasn't it at all," said Claire, placing her hand on the woman's shoulder. "Honestly, that was just chit-chat. But he does seem distressed. Maybe this whole business about my car accident. It might be flooding his emotions with reminders of his mother's terrible circumstances."

"That might be it. At least, I hope so." She pressed Claire's hand. "Thank you for listening. It's good to have another woman around. I mean, Lucy Conant is sweet as can be, but we wouldn't be able to talk like this." She pointed toward the door. "That policeman is here. I better not keep you any longer."

CHAPTER SEVENTEEN

PAUL FARROW STOOD in a corner of the study, tamping fresh tobacco into the bowl of his pipe. Lieutenant Desiata on the sofa in front of the fireplace, browsing the pages of the ocean liner book that he had picked up off the table, while David finished a call then hung up the phone.

"Quite a book you've got here, Farrow," said Desiata. "If the thought of being out on a ship two hundred miles from shore appealed to me at all, I'd give it a try." He put the book down and stood when Claire entered.

She took a seat. "Hello, Lieutenant."

Desiata dipped his head. "David tells me you're planning to go to Manhattan this morning to finalize the details of your aunt's estate."

"Yes. The attorney said the paperwork is just routine. Nothing complicated. We should be back by mid-afternoon or so."

"Let's talk about that for a minute, if you don't mind," said Desiata. "Miss Fournaris, is there anyone you can think of who might benefit from your not signing those papers?"

Claire hadn't expected such a question. She hesitated. "I … I can't imagine. There's no one left to inherit except myself and my uncle. The estate is somewhat modest—an apartment in Chicago. Some money. A few investments. Antiques. Who could possibly find that worth killing for?"

"Valuable antiques?" Desiata jotted his notes.

"A Chippendale desk, but mostly a few family heirlooms that surely wouldn't mean anything to someone other than family."

"Do you have a will?"

"Yes."

"And who inherits from you?"

"Mostly charities."

"Mostly?"

"Well, there's also a woman in my apartment building whom I help out."

"Lieutenant," said Farrow, "are we to assume from your questions that you now give credence to the idea that my niece is being stalked by a killer?"

Desiata held up the notepad. "Asking these questions helps determine whether or not there is credence."

David walked over and sat in a club chair by the fireplace. "Have you been able to learn anything more about Nurse Foge's death?"

"I don't yet have the medical examiner's final report, but it's clear that the woman suffered severe head trauma."

"What about fingerprints" Claire asked. "Did you find any on the buzzer?"

"None."

David ran his hand through his hair. "That's too bad."

Claire threw her hand out. "No, that's good. Right, Lieutenant?" She looked at Paul Farrow. "That means someone rubbed the buzzer clean. Otherwise, Marina's fingerprints would have been on it."

David looked at Desiata. "Then you think it *was* murder?" he said in a dull whisper, finally appearing stunned by what Claire had been telling him all along.

Farrow turned and paced to the other side of the room. "Good Lord!"

Desiata looked from one to the other. "But … this is important. The murderer doesn't know that we have come to that conclusion. He may still think we don't believe Miss Fournaris. That she's hysterical. That's been his goal all along— to have people think everything has been accidental. The car incident. Nurse Foge's so-called trip and fall. It's critical that there be no talk of murder with anyone, no matter how close or trusted. It must not leave this room."

"So, this button theory of Claire's," David said. "You think it's possible?"

"A woman has likely been murdered, Mr. Preisler. Anything is possible."

Claire leaned forward. "But we can now also believe that there was another murder, Leonard Kimmons."

Desiata acknowledged the remark with a slow nod. "I'm afraid so."

Claire sat, pensive. She looked up at the lieutenant. "Have you come up with any leads about H.A.?"

"Nothing yet. We're working on it." He got to his feet and circled around to the back of the sofa. "We're going to have to look at everyone and everything as far back as we can."

David lit a cigarette, then tossed the match into the hearth. "But the car accident. Would a killer deliberately drive a car off the road in the pitch dark? He'd kill himself in the process."

Desiata gave a wry grin. "Not this one. It's interesting that the path taken by the taxi after it left the road was down through a swath of woods completely clear of trees, stumps, holes, or any other major obstacle all the way to the water. And we saw evidence of some very recent small tree cuttings."

"Wait," said Claire. "I remember … as the car was swerving, there was something shiny. A marker of some kind. Remember, David? We talked about that."

"That's right. We did. Sometimes it's hard to have all the pieces immediately make sense."

"Well, they're beginning to make sense now," said Desiata. "We found a red reflector nailed to a tree at the exact point where the car entered the wooded area."

"That's bizarre."

"Better than that." Desiata tapped his pen against the notepad. "It's cunning. This killer was … is … serious. He wanted the spot clearly marked. No mistakes. And he went to a lot of trouble to make it look like an accident. Same idea with the hospital attack. If he'd managed to kill you, it would likely have been chalked up to your inability to recover from the accident. And, since he didn't kill you, you merely look like a delusional woman. Who would believe you? It worked, didn't it, Miss Fournaris?"

Claire took a deep breath. "Yes."

Farrow walked over and sat beside Claire.

"So, the killer is not only serious," she said, "he's determined."

"And the driver?" David asked. "What about him?"

"Miss Fournaris had her suspicions," said Desiata. "No one believed her. So, she went to the Kimmons' house. The man in the Kimmons' family photos was not Claire's driver." He shot a look at David. "I believe she told you that, didn't she?"

David shook his head. "I didn't know what to think, Lieutenant."

"Here's what we know so far. Kimmons was dispatched to another estate about an hour before you were to be picked up, Miss Fournaris. The call was phony. A setup. No one realized the family at that estate was still away. The person who placed the call identified himself as Morley, the family butler. But it turns out, Morley was away with the family. Kimmons went up that same road, headed to the other estate. It wasn't dark yet, so the killer was able to stand on the side in plain sight, pretending to be stranded, and wave down the limo. Once in Kimmons' limo, he killed him and dumped his body into the lake. Time of death would be harder to trace because the water was so cold, and, of course, the fractured skull would be attributed to the crash. Afterward, since Kimmons had already been on call to pick up Miss Fournaris, the killer simply drove to the train station, as Kimmons, and waited for you."

The look Desiata gave her came wrapped in a chill note of warning.

David tamped his cigarette out in the glass ashtray. "But who could this guy be?"

"We know he is capable of jumping from a moving car, able to handle the dead weight of a man. And ..." Desiata went on, "he went through a number of contrivances to make it look as though Claire was not intentionally targeted. You're perfect proof of this, David. Look how long it has taken you to even consider that what Claire was saying all along is true."

Claire shook her head. "But why me, Lieutenant?"

Desiata shrugged. "Certainly not for a relatively modest estate."

"Lieutenant, is it possible," Farrow said, "that since this killer has failed in his attempt to get Claire, he'll give it up altogether?"

"She saw him, and she survived. He didn't expect that. And even though he worked hard to keep his identity hidden, he knows it is possible that at some point, in some moment, she could identify him. He's not going anywhere."

Claire's shiver was so pronounced that Farrow took the sweater he had thrown onto a corner chair and placed it around her shoulders.

"I'm sorry. I know this is hard on you. It probably isn't going to get easier." Desiata turned one of his little notebook pages. "And I've got to consider all possibilities." He looked directly at her. "I understand you were raised by your aunt Evelyn after your mother passed away."

"Yes."

"Tell me about your father."

She looked up, her brow creased. "Why do you ask? What could he have to do with any of this? I barely knew him."

"Has he ever been in contact with you?"

She took a deep breath and looked away. "He left after my mother died. He often left. He traveled a lot. I guess what I remember most is that he was rarely around."

"Why did he leave so often?"

"He was a salesman. He traveled nearly all the time. He must have lost a lot of business during the Depression. I don't know if he even survived."

"I'm sorry for all your troubles." Desiata touched Claire's shoulder. "You've suffered a great loss."

Claire put her head in her hands. "What can I do, Lieutenant? Would it all go away if I just got on the train and went back to Chicago? Maybe my visit started all of this. Maybe if I leave…"

"I wouldn't chance it. Be cautious of anyone you don't know. And don't leave the grounds alone." Desiata put away his notebook, and turned to leave. "Your trip to Manhattan this morning is out of the question."

Claire could feel the tears building. "What on earth is happening?"

"And why is it happening?" said Farrow.

"We don't have an answer to that just yet," Desiata said.

David lit another cigarette. "Whoever this man is, Lieutenant, he's had information. He knew Claire was coming. He knew she was arriving by train and at what time. He knew when she was in the hospital. He knew about the button Marina Foge found, and that Claire was going to the nurse's apartment to get it. And he had to know that on the night of Claire's arrival, we would be unable to pick her up at the train."

Desiata gave David Preisler a thoughtful look. "How is it that you and Louis Joel were not available to pick up Miss Fournaris?"

"We took the car in for service."

"Who told you to do that?"

"Rollie Tarr."

"And who told him?"

Paul Farrow looked at Desiata. "I did. But you can't possibly think—"

"I think in all directions, Mr. Farrow. So, why didn't you pick up your niece?"

"I'd been working on the last of the drawings for the Driggs-Copeland building downtown, and I had scheduled a critical phone call with the developer before knowing the exact time of Claire's arrival. He was about to leave for London, so it wasn't a call I could reschedule."

Desiata dipped his head, then smiled. "Well, believe it or not, there is what might be considered a positive note."

"You're kidding, aren't you?" David said.

"Not at all. The fact that this murderer has staged everything as an accident indicates that he wants no one to think otherwise. Even the balcony incident. Everyone was meant to think that in the darkness and high wind, with pots blowing over, that she would accidentally have lost her balance and tumbled over the rail to her death."

"How does that help?" said Farrow.

"It means that the murderer will not use a gun or a knife or a car bomb or any other method that would indicate murder. So, as long as Claire keeps playing it safe, surrounded by trusted people, it's going to be very difficult for her to have another so-called accident."

Farrow rubbed the side of his face. "What do you think his reasoning is?"

"One guess," said Desiata, "is that in a murder case, we would have to do a lot of investigating, looking very closely at everyone. That tells me that someone is hiding something, probably something big, and this killer doesn't want it exposed. Oh, and one other thing." He stopped before opening the door to the study. "We don't even know if it's a man."

CHAPTER EIGHTEEN

WITH THE PASSING of the afternoon hours, the brightness of the day faded as did the small comfort Claire had felt knowing they finally believed her. Her spirit ached with foreboding and helplessness. She was now, in a sense, a prisoner, and even in the lighted, locked safety of the house, with two protective men at her side, and others elsewhere alerted to the danger, she wondered what mad eye might be watching from the ring of darkening woods. Was it true? She could trust no one?

There were only two for the beef bourguignon Marjorie prepared—Claire and Paul Farrow, who came to the table as casually dressed as she had yet seen him in a collegiate looking argyle sweater vest. David had gone to his apartment to collect fresh clothing, planning to return about eight or so. At Farrow's request, Marjorie set them up in the breakfast room.

It was Claire's first dinner alone with Farrow, an awkward moment, though she couldn't figure out why, especially since he had lately become more engaging. She could tell that he was just as uncomfortable as she was. Other than a few compliments on Marjorie's cooking, neither of them said much at first. Only the whispered strains of Jimmy Dorsey playing on the radio in the background and the soft clink of silverware relieved the uneasy silence. Could she blame him if he were as tired of all this madness as she was?

"I called your aunt's attorneys this afternoon," he said after a time. "I know you want Evelyn's business resolved as soon as possible. Whether Desiata will agree to your leaving when it's concluded, who knows? But let's get Evelyn's business settled, and at least put your mind at ease in that regard. I called the attorneys, explaining that there are extenuating circumstances that will prevent your going to Manhattan, and they agreed to come here in a day or two."

The first word Hannah Lillian had used to describe Paul Farrow was "kind." "Thank you," she said.

"Now, as I recall, you wanted to speak to me about something," he said, cutting another slice of the tender beef.

"Yes, well, I didn't know if I should bring it up during dinner. It's about Marina Foge's death. And Bobby Tarr."

Farrow looked surprised. "What's happened with Bobby?"

"He came to me earlier in the day, all upset about Marina's death. When Marjorie entered the room, he just let it go and walked away."

Farrow put his fork down. "That's odd."

"Marjorie had told me about his situation. About his mother, his stealing, and all. I wonder if he might be re-living the trauma of losing his mother because of everything that's been going on since I arrived."

"He shouldn't know about it beyond the fact that you had an accident. What did he say, exactly?"

"He was curious about it. How it happened. I said very little. He seemed fragile."

"I'll spend some time with him. See what's going on." He fixed his eyes on her as if in cautious evaluation. She wondered— was it the situation he was evaluating, or her? He picked up his fork, only to poke at his food and move it about the plate.

"Do you suppose we'll enter the war?" she asked.

"I believe we may have to, although I hope not. We're still getting over the last world war. Having said that, the Germans have blitzed England, especially London. And now that Japan has invaded French Indochina, Germany has formed an alliance with them and with Italy. I don't see how we can avoid it, and I'm afraid it might be a very long war."

"I've prayed that it wouldn't happen, but I think I have to agree with you,"

Then, after another awkward silence. "You know, you are the first architect I've ever met."

"Am I?"

"Yes. And I'm sometimes curious when I look at a building, how it starts out. Do you see it big as life in your mind's eye? Does it come to you bit by bit?"

"A little of both, and more. Trial and error. Sometimes, you start out with a grand vision, and by the time you get to the fifth floor, you just get on that elevator and plummet right down to the basement."

She laughed. "Well, that must be disappointing."

"Yes, it is. But, mostly, in the end, you've got something much more satisfying than not. Maybe it's because you're creating what hasn't existed before." He picked up his wine glass without sipping. "I've never been one for tall rectangles that lack character. The Chrysler building is my favorite, actually."

He went on for several minutes, fascinating her with his knowledge of buildings and a few of his favorite architects—Sullivan's Wainwright Building, the Woolworth building that Gilbert designed in 1913, Falling Water, among many others by Frank Lloyd Wright, whom he otherwise disliked as a married man running off to Europe with his married mistress. It pleased her to hear him speak of his work because he spoke with passion, and she liked the way he sounded with passion in his voice.

"I've gone on too long," he said, at last.

"Not at all. I'd like to hear more."

"Well, then, I'll share with you something that I haven't yet mentioned to anyone else. I've been asked to design an ocean liner. I've been reading up on them, wondering how like buildings they can be or might become. The Titanic held about thirty-three hundred passengers on ten decks. Knowing how our society tends to expand things, making more and more of everything, I suspect that ocean liners of the future might reach twenty decks, carrying as many as eight or ten thousand people. By then, they would seem more like villages or expansive floating resorts, with extravagant amenities we can hardly now imagine." He placed his glass on the table. "I'm being asked to dip a toe into that water, no pun intended. I'm not sure I want any part of it, since I cannot imagine a desire to travel on such a ship. And besides, who knows what the growth of air and train travel will do to ocean travel. Too many question marks. And, of course, if we do go to war, we might end up using ocean liners to transport troops. I can definitely imagine that the Queen Mary could probably hold more than ten thousand troops, crammed in as they would be. And what a rich target for the enemy. Hitler would put a bounty on that ship the moment it launched."

"I think you must be even more brilliant than Aunt Evelyn said you are."

He became quiet again, not so much as a turtle withdrawing its head as a gentleman perhaps assembling his coat of armor.

She waited.

"I imagine you miss David being at the table."

A surprising comment, out of nowhere. "Not really. I mean, he is good company…"

"But…"

"But," she laughed. "He left only an hour ago. How could I miss him so soon?"

"But you like him."

She didn't respond.

"He's extremely interested in you."

"Why do you say that?"

"I think it's obvious."

"To whom?"

He poured more of the merlot into Claire's glass, then his own. "Marjorie, for one."

"Oh?" She picked up the napkin from her lap and touched it to the corner of her mouth. "And who else?"

He didn't answer.

She took a sip of wine. "Here's what I've noticed. Even with our disagreements about all that's happened, David has become a friend, and I'm glad because I like having him as a friend." The room was comfortable and warm, the music calming, the wine a soothing tonic for the ills of the past many hours.

"I'm very grateful to David," Farrow said, "but ashamed that he's been more of a friend to you than I've been."

"How can you say that?" She knew very well how he could say that. Still… "You're family, and you have welcomed me into your beautiful home even in the midst of every craziness that I seem to have brought with me. You've sheltered me." She reached over and rested her hand on the table in front of him. "You've been very kind to me."

"So kind that I seem to have made it impossible for you to call me uncle?"

She wondered what had brought this on, why he seemed to be circling so close. Circling, circling, as Bob Lillian would say. She wondered if he would land.

Her face throbbed with heat. He was being Paul Farrow, and she was completely fascinated by him, so struck by his well-mannered, bitter-sweet reclusive oddness that she felt a kind of jealousy for Marjorie and Tarr, Patrice, and the Professor, and the others close to him who would have a place in his life long after she was gone from his house and, if not forgotten, then set neatly aside in some distant memory. Evelyn was dead, and with her passing, Paul Farrow's passing, too, since she would likely not ever see him again, the uncle she now realized never belonged to her except through the recollection of an adoring sister.

He gave her a look she had not seen before. Something about the eyes—worrisome? Apologetic? He rested his hands together in his lap and leaned in. "Claire, there is something I need to tell you. I had hoped it might become easier to say over these days since you arrived, but … it hasn't."

Her heart quickened as a new fear gripped her. She didn't respond.

He paused, watching her, then went on. "You must know how dear Evelyn was to me. At least, I hope you do."

She could only guess that to be true; there was no reason to believe otherwise. "Yes."

"You recall that before I … before *we* … Matt and I … moved here from the DC area, Evelyn came to visit."

That was more than seven, eight years ago. Claire had forgotten. Now, as she thought about it, she recalled that when her aunt returned home to Chicago, she said very little about that visit. She didn't even call Claire as soon as she got back, as she usually did after one of her travels. "Did something happen?" Her mouth went dry.

He reached for his wine glass again, and began to slowly turn it by the stem. "Yes. Something happened. And I've been—"

They turned with a start when Marjorie entered the room.

"Should I serve dessert now?"

Farrow stumbled over a response. "Uh … maybe … maybe not tonight, Marjorie." He turned to Claire, "Unless …"

"No. None for me either, Marjorie. But thank you. The dinner was wonderful."

"All right, then." She collected their dinner plates. "Oh, and David has just come in."

Claire and Farrow gave each other a look that said each understood they could not continue their conversation. "I'm sorry," he said to Claire. "Tomorrow. I promise."

Barely before the words were out, David was in the room, giving Marjorie's arm a squeeze as she exited. "Well, if they're silly enough to pass on dessert, you can count me in. All I've had is a deli sandwich and that was … who knows when." He took a seat opposite Claire.

"Then why don't I fix you a dinner plate?" Marjorie offered.

"Sounds good to me. Thank you, Marjorie." David looked from Claire to Farrow and back again. "Well, I don't know what he's promising you for tomorrow, but I hope it's better than this. You both look like the family dog died. Anything wrong?"

"Nothing more than usual," Farrow said. "There's a lot weighing on everyone."

"And tomorrow?" Preisler looked at Claire, but she remained silent, waiting on her uncle.

Farrow appeared unsettled. "Just a small lunch with the Lillian's, Patrice. One or two others. I'd forgotten."

It was true, Claire thought. Marjorie had mentioned it just before supper. Farrow appeared to dread the idea as much as Claire did, and although he had protested, Marjorie convinced him that it was just a little too late to cancel. Claire was sure that Marjorie was unaware of everything that was going on.

David unfolded his napkin. "Should be a nice weekend with the gala and all. Something to lift the spirits." He tapped Claire's wine glass with his.

Farrow put his hand on David's arm. "Just remember—we can't tell anyone what's going on, and the more people we have around, the more likely it is that something will slip out."

David straightened up as if in mild protest. "Somebody's bound to have seen the papers. That Foge died. Especially if Gomshay's coming."

"True. But Desiata has made sure there's no mention of possible homicide. We have to keep it that way."

Claire took in the two men—one so full of the energy of the moment wherever he was, and one far more enigmatic and commanding. It was clear to her that David Preisler may at times be the life of the party, but it was the gravity of Paul Farrow's presence that established the orbit of every room he entered. When Marjorie returned to the kitchen with David's dinner plate, Paul Farrow instructed her to cancel tomorrow's lunch.

"If they want to know why," he said, "say that Claire will be taking care of the business she came here to settle."

After a small glass of sherry in the study with Paul and David, Claire went to her room, vexed by the unfinished conversation with her uncle. What could possibly have happened during Evelyn's visit years back? She was grateful that Paul had made the decision to cancel the lunch. The last thing she wanted right now was a pleasant little mixer with friends, faking every smile and forcing every word, as if her world was not on fire.

She glanced at the October issue of McCall's magazine with its cute pigtailed girl helping her mother with a skein of yarn. Innocence. Sweetness. Family. What might the rest of the 1940s hold in store with the possibility of war on the horizon? She tossed the magazine onto the bed and put out the light, unaware that in the windy darkness of the woods, a lone figure in a long black coat hid among the evergreens, waiting for that perfect moment when a certain someone would meet her fate, at last.

Chapter Nineteen

Patrice Jakobiak pulled on a pair of lightweight trousers and a long-sleeved pullover, pausing with an admiring look at herself in the full-length bedroom mirror—small waist, trim but sinewy arms and legs, tall and statuesque enough, as time had proven, to attract anyone of the opposite sex. Or nearly anyone—Paul Farrow, the one stubborn hold-out. But why? They got along. They were certainly very much alike, weren't they? Both striking in a way that captured people's attention. They would have a lovely future together among the social elite. So, what was the problem? She picked up her tote with its gold embroidered insignia of the posh Shoreline Racquet Club, a place she had frequented three times a week for years. She would change into her tennis shorts and top when she got there.

She recognized, of course, that Paul Farrow had always been an introvert, more so since his niece's arrival, when everything went into disarray. But the woman certainly seemed to be recovered well enough the day before in Marjorie's kitchen. And now, at the last minute, Paul goes and cancels the little lunch he had planned at the house for today. It was clear that Claire Fournaris had a good measure of influence over her uncle, something that Patrice Jakobiak was not at all pleased about.

Arthur Jakobiak was waiting for his daughter at the bottom of the long, curved staircase, still in his bathrobe and slippers. "Good morning, my princess. You look beautiful, as always. I hurried down so I wouldn't miss you."

She kissed his cheek. "You look well this morning, Father."

"We mustn't count on it, but, yes, much better for the moment. I do think the fresh air does me good, even if one has to bundle up for it."

"Well, just make sure you're well enough for the gala. Paul's niece said she's holding you to that promise of a dance."

"That's wonderful!" He took his daughter's hand and turned her around. "I guess it pays to be a hopeless romantic."

"Well, don't overdo it, or you'll miss everything," she said, heading out the door. She'd been planning very carefully for that glitzy affair, counting on the power of her stunning black sequined, floor-length strapless—the perfect irresistible item that first kisses are made of. She slid behind the wheel, then pulled out of the four-car garage. And if that little niece of Paul Farrow's somehow manages to keep him from attending, she would scream. Better yet, she would have to strangle somebody.

Professor Jakobiak stood in the doorway, waving, as his daughter's black Bugatti Royale made its way down the circular drive. "How lucky can a man get?" He chuckled. "Claire Fournaris wants to dance with me." He heard the phone ring and, a moment later, his butler announced that Dr. Gomshay was calling.

"Thank you, Edward." Jakobiak walked to his study, where he picked up the receiver. "Well, if it isn't the man who's keeping me alive. How are you, Lyle?"

"We've got to do a bit more than keep you alive, my friend. How are you feeling today?"

"I feel good. Thinking about going into town to help with the setup for the gala."

"Now, Arthur, while we realize you're not contagious, I do think you need to rein things in a little more, or you're going to miss out on the gala altogether."

"How's my blood work?"

"Fine," said Gomshay. "A bit low on potassium. That's it."

"Well, we should be done worrying. You know I'm accustomed to an active lifestyle. I'm tired of reading, and I'm getting quite bored with Solitaire."

"I know you're accustomed to being a strong and vibrant individual, Arthur. You come and go as you please, doing whatever you choose, but at one time or another, every one of us has to slow down and pay attention to whatever the warning signs are."

Jakobiak gave out a soft chuckle. "So far, my good friend, you haven't done a very good job of showing me exactly what warning signs you're referring to."

"Well, then, do as you please, you stubborn mule, and I'll very much hope to see you at the gala. And..." There was momentary silence. "Make sure Edward keeps the doors locked."

"Why? What do you mean? What's going on?"

"Nothing, really, but Paul did mention that you came across some fellow in the woods a few days ago."

"Yes, but it was nothing. He took off as soon as he saw me. I didn't make much of it. People seem to like that little woodsy path."

"Well, don't be flip about it, Arthur. Be careful. Could be a peeping Tom. Think of Patrice."

Jakobiak let out a laugh. "Patrice? Don't worry about Patrice Jakobiak. She's stronger than both of us put together, and a jiu-jitsu master, to boot."

"Even so, better safe than sorry."

When they'd hung up, Jakobiak summoned Edward. "Is something going on around here that we should be worried about?"

"Not that I know of, Professor."

Jakobiak made his way across the great marble expanse to the curved staircase and returned to his bedroom, where he looked out at the woods, wondering.

Frank Desiata thumped the side of the station's second-floor vending machine, and, nearly a full minute later, removed a half-filled cardboard cup of black coffee before heading back to his office.

"Lieutenant," Sergeant Greeley called out. "Got something on the Fournaris case."

"You're sure about this?" Desiata said, after looking over the file.

"Talked with the medical examiner. No question that the blow that killed her is too high on the head." Greeley pointed to the photos. "You can see the position of the body."

"Face down," said Desiata. "She wouldn't have suffered that kind of a blow falling forward."

"Hit from behind. Someone tall," said Greeley. "Oh, and here's the other information you wanted." He placed another file on the desk. "You have good instincts, Frank."

Desiata took a sip of coffee and began looking through the pages of information Greeley had compiled—a couple of group photos, several magazine and journal clippings, and a copy of a short, years-old Page 3 newspaper piece that raised Desiata's eyebrows. "Get hold of Paul Farrow. I'll need to go out there this afternoon and talk to him and his niece."

Chapter Twenty

"WELL, SINCE YOU'RE stuck here anyway," said David, "how about letting me accompany you to the gala this weekend?" He and Claire were having lunch as Marjorie rolled out dough on the large wooden prep table at the far end of the kitchen. There were several places in Paul Farrow's beautiful house where Claire had come to feel completely at home, none more than Marjorie's large, welcoming kitchen, with its black and white checkered-tile floor, red-gingham valances, antique pie cupboard, and open shelves filled with an assortment of colorful canisters, bowls, and serving platters, along with two large roll-top breadboxes. Claire loved the handsome vintage stove, and the enormous prep table covered with flour for kneading, sandwich makings, or peels of one kind or another.

"What do you think, Marjorie? She should let me take her, right?"

"I think she should make her own decisions," Marjorie said, sinking her fingers into a mound of pastry dough.

Claire tapped David with her foot under the table to alert him to be careful about what they discussed in front of Marjorie. "I don't know that I'll be able to go, David. You know. I really should stay here."

"Oh, well now," said Marjorie, "no point missing such a wonderful evening out. Personally, I think it would do you good to be around more people. It might be fun."

A few minutes later, when Marjorie had set her dough aside to rise, and stepped out of the kitchen, Claire leaned toward David. "You know I'm not supposed to go anywhere."

David took a sip of coffee then set his cup down. "That's not what the lieutenant said. He said not to go to Manhattan."

"He said not to leave the grounds."

"It's okay if you're with one of us. There's a big difference. There'll be about two hundred people at the gala. And nearly everyone there will know nearly everyone else who's there. Besides, I'll be with you. And so will your uncle, along with the friends you've met here so far." He reached over and touched her hand. "You'll be as safe as if you were right here at the house. And once Paul hears that you've agreed to go, you can be sure he'll have Parmalee and Louis go, too, as a kind of silent back-up security."

It crossed her mind that David might be right. It could be a good change of pace to be at such a festive event. "I … I don't even have a proper dress … a gown, or something appropriate."

"An easy fix," David said. He got up from the table just as Paul Farrow came into the kitchen.

"What fix is that?" Farrow asked.

"Taking your stubborn niece into town to get a dress for the gala."

Claire felt self-conscious. "I wasn't sure if I'm allowed to go."

Farrow hesitated. "I … don't see why not." He poured himself a cup of coffee. "It's about as safe a place as any. Lots of people knowing lots of other people. Might be good for you. Might be good for all of us."

Claire was glad to hear it, but, at the moment, there was something else she needed to know from her uncle. "Will we have a chance to … you know … talk today?"

"I looked for you earlier."

"Oh, I'm sorry," she said. "I was enjoying a book in the sunroom."

David shot a look from one to the other. "On that happy note, I think I'll get some business done."

"Why don't we go to my study?" Farrow said after David left the kitchen. "Desiata wants to come this afternoon. I hope we have time before he gets here."

As the two headed out of the small private corridor from the kitchen, they saw Rollie Tarr hurrying across the main floor. "Sorry to bother, but the lieutenant is here, Mr. Farrow. He's in the study."

Farrow looked at his watch. "He's early."

Just as the three greeted each other in the study, the phone rang, and Farrow answered it, listening for a moment in silence, his brow crimped. "I don't understand how this could possibly happen," Farrow said to the caller. "We'll be right there." When he ended the call, he ran his hand through his hair. "Lieutenant, please forgive me. That was the care facility where Matthew is.

They found him on the grass outside one of the doors. Without his wheelchair."

"Sorry to hear that," Desiata said. "I thought he was incapacitated."

"So, did I," said Farrow. "Could we please reschedule for later today or tomorrow?"

"If it's possible to make it later today," said the lieutenant, "that would be best. There are a few things that have come up."

When Paul Farrow and Edmund Parmalee arrived at the care center, they were astonished to find Matthew sitting on the edge of his bed, one of the attendants in a chair next to him. As soon as the two men greeted the patient, he called out "Vee. Vee."

"What does that mean?" the attendant asked. "He's been saying it all morning. He says it often. We believe it was somehow instrumental in his getting out of his chair."

"But how could he?" Parmalee asked. "This man has not been able to walk for more than six years?"

"Are you sure about that?" said the attendant. "He's very strong. It took three of us to restrain him once we got him to his feet."

"Strange," said Farrow.

After a brief visit during which Matthew had returned to his very private far-away place, Farrow and Parmalee headed back home with the assurance that he would be closely monitored. It was nearly four.

As Tarr took their hats and coats, Claire came hurrying across the great room. "Is Matthew all right?"

"He'll be fine," said Farrow, not wishing to offer details that might be disturbing to her.

"I'm so glad to hear that," she said.

"Has Desiata returned?"

"Just minutes ago. He's in the study."

CHAPTER
TWENTY-ONE

MARJORIE BROUGHT A tea tray into Farrow's study, then left as Farrow poured a cup for Claire, for the lieutenant, and, finally, one for himself.

"I feel so anxious about what you might have discovered," Claire said.

Desiata stared into his teacup for a moment. "Your feelings are well-founded, Miss Fournaris. What I have to share is going to be … at the very least … unsettling."

Claire sat on the edge of her chair like a nervous child, certain that if she were to open her mouth to speak, the sound of her heartbeat would bounce off every wall in Paul Farrow's study.

Desiata looked at Farrow, then at Claire. "I've heard from the medical examiner. It was as I suspected. The blow to the head that caused the fatal blunt force trauma came from behind, from a taller person, and at an angle too high on the head to be caused by the fall forward as was originally determined."

Claire was still holding onto her teacup without taking a sip. "So, Marina Foge was actually murdered."

Desiata hesitated. "Well, yes, she was." He placed his cup on the side table and got to his feet. "But I wasn't talking about Marina Foge."

"Wait," Claire said. "Are you telling us there's been another murder?"

"Yes, I am."

"Oh, my Lord," said Farrow, as he put his cup down and took a seat next to Claire on the sofa.

"This one happened about a month or so ago," Desiata said. He reached down and took Claire's cup from her hands, leaving her with a puzzled look. She turned to Farrow, who appeared as confused as she did.

Desiata stood in front of Claire. "The person I'm referring to is … Evelyn Farrow."

"What?" The word shot out of Claire's mouth on a small burst of laughter, before she realized that the lieutenant had not changed expression. She kept her eyes on him, waiting for something—a correction: not her aunt. What did Evelyn have to do with any of this? It was Marina Foge. That's who was murdered. "What are you talking about?"

Paul Farrow took Claire's hand, but she pulled it from him and shot to her feet. "What kind of a terrible … horrible … joke is this? How can you … how can you…?"

Desiata put his hand on her shoulder. "It is no joke, Miss Fournaris. I promise you."

"What are your promises worth? You don't know anything. You can't do anything. This ridiculous … this crazy idea about my aunt. How could you even suggest such a thing?" Claire had backed away from both men, backward toward the bookcases until she bumped into one of the shelves, and threw her hands to her face. "Oh, my God. Aunt Evelyn."

Farrow went to her and put his arm around her. "Lieutenant, are you absolutely certain of this?"

Claire sobbed, barely able to get the words out. "This can't … be. It … just can't."

Farrow removed the white handkerchief from his back trouser pocket and pressed it softly to Claire's face. "Let's find out about this," he said. "Let's see what the lieutenant has to say."

"This is one piece of news I would never have wanted to deliver," Desiata said.

Claire lifted her tear-streaked face, her eyes now swollen and red. "Then why do it? How do you know? How can it be? Aunt Evelyn. Please, not Aunt Evelyn."

Farrow led Claire to the sofa and sat beside her. He picked up her teacup. "Please, Claire, take a sip."

She slowly pushed his hand away as the lieutenant pulled one of the side chairs closer to them. "Would it be okay if I explained, Miss Fournaris? Or … if it's at all easier for you, I could come back tomorrow."

"No," Claire said, her voice quiet and direct. "Tell me now, Lieutenant." She turned to Farrow. "He should tell us now. She was your sister."

Farrow gave a grim nod. "However you want us to handle this, Claire."

Claire blotted her face with the handkerchief, then fidgeted with it as she trained her eyes on Desiata. "Then, tell us."

"It was something you said a few days ago, Miss Fournaris, when you mentioned your aunt's passing. It didn't seem especially significant to me at that moment, the fact that she was found with her foot looped in the venetian blind cord."

Claire searched Desiata's face, stunned, then turned to Farrow. "Lord, have mercy. The same. It's the same. A cord around the ankle."

"Those words came to me, Miss Fournaris, as I was thinking about Marina Foge's situation. Coincidence? I thought it might be. But after all that you've been experiencing here, all that's happened, I searched it out." Desiata clasped his hands in front of him. "I got in touch with the police department in downtown Cincinnati, knowing they would have made a report, since it happened at one of their big local hotels. Every incident of this kind has to be investigated, in any case. The fact of the matter is that the medical examiner there made a wrong assumption. It can happen. They have many pressing cases. Still, he accepted too quickly and with too much finality that your aunt had fallen. I insisted he revisit the physical evidence of that so-called fall. He was shocked by what he discovered, what had been overlooked. It didn't take long for me to connect the two incidents."

Claire put her head in her hands and sobbed. "It's like losing her all over again … only … only this time … even more horrible. Just horrible."

Desiata stood. "I am very sorry, Miss Fournaris," He looked at Farrow. "For both of you. I can only imagine what a great shock this is. I will see you in a day or so to answer whatever questions you have and to update you on anything I discover. And, of course, you can call me at any time. Right now, I'm still looking into both situations. They will continue to be a top priority." He pulled the chair back to where it belonged. "I'll show myself out." When he reached the door of the study, he turned. "Oh. Once again, please keep this to yourselves. It will be safer that way."

Long after Lieutenant Desiata left, Claire was inconsolable. Farrow had locked the door to the study, which everyone in the household understood to mean that he did not wish to be disturbed. Beaten down by the shocking news and the flood of tears that accompanied her fresh grief, Claire succumbed to her exhaustion, resting against the arm of the sofa, asleep. Farrow put a pillow under her head and placed a coverlet over her, then sat for a long time near the fire watching her. How much more would Desiata uncover? Farrow put his head back and thought about the possibilities with great discomfort, before he himself could no longer keep his eyes open.

Chapter Twenty-Two

ON THURSDAY AFTERNOON, the grand ballroom at the Regent Crown Hotel in Westport, Connecticut, teemed with a lively scramble of gala volunteers crisscrossing the expanse with a fabulous variety of decorative accessories, from ornamental swags and banners to gilded floor easels that would hold the posters heralding the achievements of Arthur Jakobiak's Center for the Enrichment of Mankind (CFEM). While hotel workmen on scaffolds threaded the enormous chandeliers with glittering gold and crystal vines, volunteers on stage arranged the seating for the twenty-five-piece Ken Healy Orchestra. More would be done over the next two days, the last of which, on Saturday afternoon when the spectacular orchid arrangements for the twenty-five table rounds and the three-dozen potted ficus and fiddle leaf fig floor plants would be set in place.

In a rare private moment, Lucy Conant managed to take Hannah Lillian and Patrice Jakobiak aside. "Does anyone know what's going on at Paul's? David is all gloom. Everyone's walking around like … I don't know … like someone died.

That police lieutenant was there again, more than once, and I haven't seen Claire for two days."

"I wonder if it has anything to do with Lyle's nurse who died," said Hannah. "I understand Claire and David arrived right after the accident."

"Maybe so," said Lucy. "David said it was awful, and Claire's certainly been through a lot, hasn't she?"

Patrice shrugged. "She would have been better off going home right after she got out of the hospital following her car accident. Her aunt's lawyers could have found another way to finalize things."

Hannah Lillian touched Patrice's arm. "Your father is about as close as anyone is to Paul. Has he said anything?"

"Nothing," said Patrice. "Paul Farrow is supposed to be at the gala to accept my father's award. That's all he cares about. As for me, I'm done caring about any of it. Tonight's the gala and I plan to have a lovely time … with or without the enigmatic Mr. Farrow and his adorable, star-crossed niece."

The three turned to see the professor coming across the room.

"Well, look who's here," said Hannah, with a laugh in her voice.

"That's my dad," Patrice said with amiable resignation. "He said he wanted to stop by just to see how everything's going."

Jakobiak greeted everyone in his path along the way. "Ah, this is wonderful."

"Yes, it certainly is," said Hannah. "Too bad that you, of all people, are going to miss it. First time ever."

"Well, don't count me out just yet."

Hannah pressed her fingers to her chin. "Well, you might not do so well, my friend, if you don't stay out of the cold and wind."

"Professor," said Lucy Conant, "we were wondering if you know anything about what's going on at Paul's. It's like a graveyard, and that police lieutenant keeps coming and going."

"Can't say that I do." Jakobiak pressed his lips together. "I saw his niece on the terrace once or twice. We waved to each other. She did seem a bit unenthusiastic, but I don't know why." He crimped his brow. "Haven't seen much of Paul or David, or any of them, for that matter, just Louis out polishing the cars. And Rollie rushing here and there doing his usual this or that. I only wish my man, Edward, were as attentive and industrious. He always seems to be missing, somehow. I can't imagine where he goes or what he's up to. In any case, as far as Farrow goes, I imagine the police are still investigating that car accident. After all, the driver drowned." He shook his head. "That poor young woman is lucky to be alive."

"And what are you doing outside when it's so cold and windy?" Hannah said. "One of these days Gomshay is going to put you in the hospital, and missing the gala will be the least of your problems."

"Please let us know if you hear anything, Professor," said Lucy.

"You'll be the first." He gave a polite dip of his head. "Now, I must go and give just a little guidance here and there." He pointed toward the stage. "I see that poster needs to be moved a little to the left," he said, walking into the noisy bustle, smiling, and calling out his directions with likeable authority.

Evelyn Farrow's attorneys had been prompt and expedient that morning, arriving at ten and gone by eleven—a few signatures and a witness. They had managed to validate Claire's identification and bank access, which included transfer of all funds from her aunt's accounts and the key to her safe deposit box in Chicago, along with the title to Evelyn's apartment.

When they were gone, Claire went immediately to the sunroom at the far end of the main floor, where she surprised Bobby Tarr, who jumped when she entered.

"I'm so sorry, Bobby. I … I didn't mean to …

"It's okay," he said. "I was just …" And without finishing, he let himself out through the side door that opened onto a large grassy area and garden off the far-end of the drive near the garage. She didn't hear Paul Farrow enter the sunroom.

"Glad to see you," he said, causing her to jump. "So sorry."

"It's okay," she said.

"Haven't seen you in two days. How are you doing? You look well."

She took a deep breath. "I can't imagine how that can be true, but thank you for saying it. I also want to thank you for

… for the pillow and blanket the other night. The lieutenant's news knocked me for a loop. I still can't believe it."

"It shocked us both." Farrow thumped the bowl of his pipe against his palm, then set it in the ashtray. "Desiata needs to see us in his office."

She rubbed her forehead. "Oh, how I want to be done with all this. All of it."

"I understand how hard this has been."

"When does he want to see us?"

"As soon as possible," Farrow said. "And besides, the sun is out. Even a blip of warm air on your face could do you a world of good. You agree?"

"I suppose so," she said. And they got their coats and hats.

"Where are we?" Claire shielded her eyes from the blinding glare of the afternoon sun.

"I'm taking the long route," Farrow said.

Ten minutes later, as they cruised a winding road much too far out of town for

police headquarters, Desiata's warning shot through her thoughts—"Trust no one." She touched his arm. "Paul, please. I'm … I don't know where you're taking me."

In a small roadside clearing along the shoulder, Farrow pulled the car over, then shifted to look directly at her. "You're scared," he said, surprised. "I'm so sorry. I wanted this to be a little outing. Something to help lift your spirits. I knew that if I asked you to go for a ride in the country, you would have said no. You've been hiding out for two days."

She sat silent for a moment, staring straight ahead.

"I'll turn the car around if that's what you want."

"Maybe you're right—a ride in the country could be good. For both of us."

"I thought we could stop up ahead for lunch. Marjorie says you haven't been eating much of anything. There's also a pumpkin farm farther along. We can pick out a pumpkin. What do you say?"

"Well … if you don't mind the poor company, the only thing I can say is thank you."

An hour later, the waitress brought dessert—a slice of warm apple pie topped with a slice of cheddar cheese. Claire sat back, more relaxed than she imagined she could feel. "This place must be even more beautiful in summer."

Farrow looked through the French cottage windows at the golden maples that flanked a narrow stream. "That it is," he said. Neither one said another word until the waitress refilled their coffee cups. "Feel like talking about it?"

She dipped her head, then looked up at him. "I … just don't know how to make sense of any of it, Paul. Evelyn murdered. Two others. And whoever did these … these horrible things, wants me dead too." She picked at her fingers. "And where would he stop? How many others is he willing to kill to get to me, or even after me? And for what reason?"

"The only positive thing I can offer is that Lieutenant Desiata is on it, and I'm beginning to see that he's better at all of this than I first gave him credit for." He picked up her fork and handed it to her. "Now, finish your apple pie. There's a big, beautiful pumpkin waiting for us."

Two hours later, with the largest pumpkin the two could lift into the trunk of the Cadillac, Tarr came dashing out of the front door of the house. "Oh, perfect timing, Miss Fournaris. Marjorie has someone on the phone for you."

"For me?" Claire said, hurrying into the house. "Who on earth could it be?"

Chapter Twenty-Three

Marjorie held the phone out as Claire hurried in. "A woman. I believe she said Shipman."

"Abigail Shipman? Of all people." Claire took the phone.

"Claire, dear," came the doleful voice. "I only just heard. Late last night. I am so sorry. I'm in shock. You must be devastated."

Abigail Shipman, long-time colleague of Evelyn Farrow, had moved in the same professional circles, often attending the same conferences and sharing an occasional board membership or committee chair. Taken in tolerable doses, the woman was someone Evelyn occasionally liked and admired. The feeling was mutual, both women aware that their relationship benefited from the considerable geographical distance between them— opposite ends of half the country. Everyone knew the woman to be a somewhat well-intentioned and sincere person with a dogged enthusiasm for gossip. Who could ever trust that they would not soon be the next one whose name was on the tip of her tongue?

"Thank you, Abby. It was a shock to us all. How on earth did you know where to reach me?"

"It wasn't easy. Your aunt had given me your home address and phone number a long time ago, in case I ever had difficulty reaching her at home. So, when there was no answer at your apartment, I managed to find your landlady. Of course, she was quite reluctant to tell me anything, as she should be, but I believe she sensed how genuinely distraught I was over our dear Evelyn's passing. Please don't be hard on her when you get back home."

"I wouldn't think of it, Abby. I appreciate your call. You knew my aunt for many years."

Paul Farrow busied himself with small tasks about the kitchen, now and then looking over at Claire while drying the same teacup over and over. Claire shrugged to indicate that there was no great urgency in the call, nothing to worry about. She nearly laughed when he absent-mindedly ran the same cup under hot water and started drying it all over again.

"Oh, well, I just had to track you down to let you know that Harman and I would have been there for the services, if only we had known. We've been away since the convention … actually, since just before the convention ended. I hated to cut it short, but that's the only time of year that Harman can be away at a stretch, and we had so been looking forward to this extended vacation in the British Isles. We sailed out of New York for Southampton. I wasn't quite ready to fly all the way to England but, well, I know I'll have to get used to it sooner or later. It's 1940 after all." She laughed.

"All in all, it sounds like a wonderful trip."

"Oh, it was, Claire. We arrived home early last evening. That's when I started going through the stack of mail and came across the Association newsletter. You could have knocked me over with a feather when I saw your aunt's sweet face, right there on page one. And those ghastly headlines. "'Freak accident claims life at Cincinnati convention site.'"

The words were chilling. "It must have been very upsetting for you," Claire offered, "especially since you had just seen her at the convention."

"Yes, very upsetting. And to think—I might have been the last person to see your aunt alive. Well, myself and her visitor."

"Visitor?"

"Yes, the person who was with her in her room when I stopped to say goodbye."

Claire felt her heart drop. Evelyn had never been one to socialize much at these conventions, let alone inviting someone to her hotel room. She liked her privacy as well as time away from the crowds and the noise, and it bothered her that some people just didn't know when to leave. "Could you tell who it was?"

Paul Farrow stopped wiping the teacup and turned to lean against the counter.

"I didn't get a good look. All I could see was the long coat, like he … or she … had either just arrived or was just about to leave."

"So, you never found out who it was?"

"No. And from the way it appeared, I wasn't meant to."

Claire's hands were shaking. She and Farrow locked eyes. "Why is that?"

Farrow stepped closer and leaned against the large table.

Abby Shipman began speaking in a loud whisper, as if the best gossip shouldn't be spoken out loud. "Only because … well … you know … if there's a man in your room …"

"Are you sure it was a man?"

"Actually, no."

"About what time was that?"

"Seven. I know because Harman and I were on a tight travel schedule, and I just couldn't leave without seeing Evelyn. So, I knocked, and—funny thing—when your aunt opened the door, this person, whoever it was, turned quickly away as if they didn't want to be seen."

Claire motioned for Farrow to come close to the phone so he could hear. "That's odd."

"I thought so, too. She said she thought it was room service. She must have known the person in the room well enough to order up room service. In any event, your aunt stepped out and walked me backward into the corridor, closing the door partway behind her."

Farrow raised his eyebrows.

Claire twisted the phone cord in her hand. "And you couldn't tell who it was? Man or woman?"

"I got such a brief look. And even if I did see who it was, I may not have known them anyway. I can't possibly know everyone in the association and certainly not all the new members." Abby Shipman sighed loudly into the phone. "Oh, dear. This is not the conversation I intended to have with you, Claire. I only wanted to—"

"I know, Abby. And I am very grateful for your call and your concern. I wonder. Would you do me a favor? Would you please send me the convention list—all the names and phone numbers of every person who attended, even the exhibitors. I know it's an odd request, since I'm not a member, but I'd like to have it as soon as possible, so I can … you know … get in touch with the people who sent such wonderful remembrances."

Farrow gave her a wink for quick thinking.

"A lovely idea," said Abigail Shipman. "I'll be sure to send it by overnight courier. You'll have it Saturday."

Amid the belated condolences, Abigail Shipman had innocently delivered a charge no smaller than the A-bomb. When they finally ended the call, Claire was trembling so much that Farrow had to help her unwrap her hand from the receiver. She couldn't help noticing the scent of his aftershave, the depth of his eyes. After Farrow led her to a seat at the kitchen table, he poured her a glass of water, and they sat together, both having only one word in mind, one name—Desiata.

Chapter Twenty-Four

"Are you sure, Lucy?" Claire asked. "The gala is tonight. I don't want to keep you from helping them get ready. It's almost noon."

Lucy Conant took the six pages of convention attendees that Claire handed her and smiled. "The gala has so many volunteers." She glanced at the kitchen clock. "It's barely noon, and I'm not due to help out at the hotel until three. Now," she said, with amiable resolve, "what would you like me to do?"

"Okay." Claire handed her a red pen. "Just put a check mark next to any name whose initials would be H. A."

"Got it."

A few minutes later, Claire noticed that Lucy had gotten it backwards—she had begun checking names beginning with A. "Oh, Lucy. I'm sorry. I guess I didn't make myself clear. It's H.A., as in, let's say, Howard Anderson."

"Oh, sorry. I misunderstood."

When Lucy had finished and gone, Claire gathered up her pages and put them in the stack behind hers. With more than thirty-five-hundred names, there was still a long way to go, and if she was planning to attend the gala, as everyone in the household had insisted, the remainder of the list would have to be put aside.

Claire paused in front of the full-length mirror, surprised by the beauty and extravagance of her radiant blue silk Crepe de Chine gown and the white chinchilla cape covering her bare shoulders. Paul Farrow's generosity had no bounds. She had felt guilty until she remembered Evelyn's advice: *Don't ever waste a single moment that carries the potential for happiness.* At least the gala had the potential to eclipse, even temporarily, all the recent moments of shattering darkness. And for that, she would allow herself the luxury of gratitude, if not pure joy.

David went to her as soon as she reached the bottom of the staircase. "Claire Fournaris, you look glorious." Paul Farrow, also in tuxedo, stood off to the side, smiling his agreement. As David took her arm and led her to the door, she looked back toward Farrow.

"I'll be taking us, Claire," Farrow said, as if responding to her inquisitive look. "Louis and Parmalee will go in David's car."

"It all sounds wonderful," Claire said. "I'm trying not to feel guilty."

"No guilt tonight, my beauty," said David. "Let this be a kind of breakthrough occasion—all that is past is past."

Oh, how she wanted that to be true and to feel it all the way to her bones, but was he forgetting that there was a murderer on the loose, with her as his target?

"David is right," Farrow offered, without taking his eyes off the road. "You really do look lovely. I hope it's a good evening for you. You deserve it."

In the dull illumination of the dashboard and the fragmented light from the occasional street lamp, she was unable to read his expression. "I don't know what to say or how to thank you."

"No need."

"You've been so generous."

"Happy to accommodate." He finally glanced her way. "I know David is elated."

Ahh. David, again. Could Paul Farrow be jealous? She had first picked up on this at supper a few nights before. Now, without understanding how such a thing could possibly slip out, she said, "I was hoping you would be, too." He looked at her again. And from that moment, she sat frozen in silence.

CHAPTER
TWENTY-FIVE

THE REGENT CROWN was alive, glamorous, joyful. Claire found herself uplifted by the glitter and the noise—orchids on every table, laughter, orchestra music, dancing as she hadn't seen in … how long had it been? She had forgotten. But she wanted to get lost in all of it.

At the first slow song following their fabulous Beef Wellington dinner, David rose from their table of eight and took Claire's hand. "This one's for us." He led her onto the dance floor amid the dreamy strains of "You Made Me Love You." With nearly two hundred people in attendance, the dance floor was happily congested, everyone obviously taking the evening to heart, bumping lightly into others, drawing deeper into each other's arms.

"It looks like your niece has a suitor," Miriam Gomshay said, as she and Paul Farrow enjoyed a foxtrot.

"If that's what she wants," Farrow said, before Patrice Jakobiak cut in.

"I'm sorry, dear Miriam, but I need to take this gentleman off your hands," she said, passing the woman off to Bud Thomas.

David Preisler drew Claire closer. "Glad you came?"

"It's a beautiful evening."

"I was hoping for something a little more personal."

Claire offered a smile in response, more than grateful for the diversion the evening provided. She danced as she hadn't in years, engaged in lively conversations with her new friends, shared fond recollections of Evelyn, and accepted invitations for lunch and shopping.

She also enjoyed a little too much of her first champagne in years, applauded along with the crowd for Paul Farrow's speech in accepting the professor's award. She did the tango with Bob Lillian, a slow dance with Lyle Gomshay and, later, with Bud Thomas, and had her very first meeting with the elegant professor himself, who arrived late into the evening. Paul Farrow gave them a formal introduction before the professor took Claire's hand for a waltz.

Claire was surprised to find her uncle's good friend a far more robust gentleman than she had expected, considering his recent health challenges. He was also far more gracious than his daughter, and not in the least as haughty.

"So honored to meet you, Professor."

"Please call me Arthur. 'Professor' is much too formal when I'm in the company of someone as lovely as you. You're everything I imagined Paul Farrow's niece to look like … and more."

"You must be very proud of your foundation." She gestured to the fullness of the room. "It's clear that everyone else is. I know Evelyn was. She spoke of you often."

"Thank you for saying so, dear Claire. The foundation has become my life, really." He stood back and held her out at arm's length. "But … I'm not here to talk about me. I'm here to fill the rest of your dance card."

"I believe I've had a little too much champagne," she laughed, a bit lightheaded.

"In that case, I need to join you," he said as they returned to the table.

"Sorry, Arthur," Farrow said, taking Claire's arm. "Our princess's carriage awaits."

"Leaving so soon?" David said to Farrow. "I can take Claire home."

"So can I," said Jakobiak.

Farrow looked at his watch. "It's after midnight, so I guess I'm fulfilling my duty as a responsible uncle." When they had said their goodnights, Farrow led Claire to the hotel lobby, where he collected his coat and wrapped the white fur cape around her shoulders, as she pulled on her long white gloves.

She looked up at him, a bit unsteady on her feet. "We … we could stay, you know. You haven't even danced with me. But I've had such a good time."

"I can tell," he said, a touch of laughter in his voice.

She thanked him again. And less than half a mile along, she fell asleep, her head resting against his arm.

Chapter Twenty-Six

It was early Sunday afternoon when Claire emerged from her room and managed to navigate the winding staircase, each jarring motion a further assault on her aching head. The house was quiet, the only sign of life a note from Paul Farrow on the refrigerator door. "Hey, Sleepy Head, Marjorie and Tarr are out with Bobby. Louis is off today. You'll find a wonderful cold chicken plate in the refrigerator, and I've left you a thermos of hot coffee on the counter. Muffins in the bread box. Parmalee and I have gone to see Matthew. You're not alone—David is there. Please don't leave the house."

Holding onto her cup of coffee with both hands, she trekked with cautious steps to the sun room at the far end of the main floor, barely making it through the door, before her tender eyes could not cope with the glare. She retreated to Paul Farrow's study, where the coziness of the hearth welcomed her into the room. "Oh, thank you, Lord. Thank you," she uttered, taking a seat by the fire.

David Preisler found her there. "Well, it's about time."

"Please don't yell, David."

"Oh, I didn't realize I was yelling." he said, with an exaggerated whisper. "You were wonderful last night."

"It was nice."

"May I take you to breakfast?"

"Do I look like someone who's prepared to have the world see what a wretch I am?"

"You're beautiful. I told you so last night. And … I'll tell you again right now. I'm serious about this."

She squinted him into focus. "About what?"

"Us."

"Us?"

"Don't tell me you don't know that I'm crazy about you. Let me take you out. A leisurely Sunday ride in the country. I promise to drive slowly, speak quietly, and keep you safe. It will be fun."

"Do you not see that I am in the late stages of death by fun? This should be good news for my murderer friend—he can give up trying to kill me. I'm doing it for him."

David could see from her grimace that his laughter must have pierced her brain like a spike. "Oh, I'm sorry," he whispered again. "So sorry."

"Well, then, go away," she whispered.

"I can't. I'm the one who's here to keep you safe. Technically, I'm on duty. You can't send me away."

"Then, just sit there quietly and pretend you are not here. I will do the same."

Paul Farrow and Edmund Parmalee arrived home a little after four, their hands filled with cartons of take-out from Lum's Chinese restaurant in town. Claire felt much better after taking a nap. And over egg rolls and chop suey in the kitchen, she apologized to David for being a horrible person, which only brought laughter from the others.

"How was Matthew today?" she asked.

"About the same as usual."

Parmalee dropped a handful of crispy Chinese noodles into his wonton soup. "But this time, no more wandering about. And they still can't figure out how he made it into the yard that one day. Baffling."

Farrow studied Claire. "You made quite an impression on everyone last night."

She looked down at her plate of food, self-conscious. "I hope I didn't embarrass anyone."

"Not a chance," said Farrow. "It was good to see you enjoying yourself. We hadn't seen that side of you before."

David agreed. "It's clear that the professor was taken with you."

"In fact," said Farrow, "Patrice has invited us for dinner Wednesday night."

Claire looked about the table, amazed by this small collection of people she now felt so close to, people she didn't even know a few weeks before. She felt safe but also welcomed, and cared for, and liked. "Are you sure it's okay for me to show my face?"

"They love you," said Farrow. "Besides, everyone else enjoyed the champagne about as much as you did."

"I must admit," she said, "I hadn't danced that much in such a long time."

David held up his cup of hot tea as a toast. "Well, then, here's to much more dancing. There's a great little supper club along Shoreline …"

"Hold on, David," said Farrow. "I don't want to put a damper on things, but let's not forget that we've got a serious problem. So, for now, let's just count on having a good time at the Jakobiak's dinner party on Wednesday, where we'll be among friends." He put his fork down. "In the meantime, I have a feeling we're going to be seeing more of our lieutenant friend, and we have no idea what he's going to come up with next."

CHAPTER
TWENTY-SEVEN

PAUL FARROW COULDN'T have guessed how right he was. Lieutenant Desiata was on the phone first thing Monday morning with a request to see him in his office by noon.

"Should I bring Claire?"

"No."

There was a stern edge to Desiata's voice that Farrow had not detected before, and that tone matched the look on his face when Farrow entered the lieutenant's office around eleven.

"Have a seat."

Farrow removed his hat and coat and tossed them onto a side chair. "Has something happened? You're looking more serious than I've seen you. It must be—"

"Serious? It's serious. Yes," said Desiata, taking the seat behind his desk, after closing the door to his office.

Farrow appeared confused. "What's going on?"

Desiata began tapping a pencil nonchalantly against his desk blotter. "How long did you expect to keep this up?"

"Keep what up? I don't understand."

"I'll give you time to think," said Desiata, his eyes locked on the man in front of him.

Farrow looked away, lacing his fingers in front of him, without responding.

"I told you that I would be looking at this case from all angles."

Farrow looked at Desiata with a flick of his eye. "And?"

"Tell me about Matthew Ettinger."

Farrow shifted in his seat. "What is there to tell? You've seen him."

"Oh, yes, I certainly have. And from what I've discovered, there is much to tell." Desiata sat back and rested his hands on the arms of his chair. "For one thing, I've looked into your finances." The lights flickered as the October gusts beat against the windows of the station house.

"I knew you would be thorough, Lieutenant. It's one of the things I admire most about you. Tell me, what is it, exactly, that you have discovered regarding my finances?"

"That every dollar you spend comes from Matthew Ettinger's account. How long did you think you would get away with this?"

Farrow's response was immediate and angry. "Nothing I've ever done has been about getting away with anything. I've had nothing to gain." He got to his feet and turned for the door. "Since you seem to know so much, Lieutenant, there's nothing more I need to tell you, is there? Except this—I am and will continue to be the caretaker of my dear and loyal friend of many years."

"And … what about Miss Fournaris?"

He drew his head back. "What about Claire? What has she got to do with this? She came to settle a business matter. Someone has tried to kill her. He's still trying. He's killed others. I suggest, Lieutenant, that your time be more gainfully spent finding this maniac."

"In due time," said Desiata, "Sometimes, it's the person you least expect."

For a while, the two men sat in silence. Then, Desiata came around and leaned against the front of his desk. "I know more than you think I know. So, why don't you tell me? Start from the beginning."

Farrow remained silent, without expression.

"You realize Miss Fournaris is going to have to know."

Farrow looked up. "I tried telling her last week, but we were interrupted. Then, the news about her aunt's murder seemed to make it impossible to burden her with one more thing."

"Why don't we go home now? And you can tell us both." He put a hand on Farrow's shoulder. "I have a feeling this is a story too painful for you to tell more than once."

Claire Fournaris looked at the two men. "You both look so … serious. You're scaring me. Has something happened?"

They were in the study, doors locked. They would not want to be disturbed.

"Remember I said there was something I needed to tell you, Claire?"

She nodded.

"Actually, I tried to tell you several times, but …"

"I'm frightened, Paul. Lieutenant, what's going on?"

"Your … uncle … will explain."

"Well, to start with. I …" Farrow turned and leaned over the fireplace with both hands on the mantle. "I … am not your uncle."

Claire let out a nervous laugh. "What are you talking about?"

"I am not Paul Farrow. I am, in fact, Matthew Ettinger."

Claire sat, speechless. She looked from one to the other for something that could possibly have this make sense, or prove it to be untrue. A mistake. A bad joke.

Desiata moved to the sofa to sit beside Claire. "We know this comes as a shock."

"A shock? Are you kidding? This is madness." She stood, her body rigid.

"Claire," Desiata said. "You know that I've had to do a lot of digging. More times than we realize, the most unexpected things show up. Sometimes, as now, they are things that are very hard to believe or accept."

"Then, you're serious." Claire trained her eyes on Farrow. "But how can this be? You're my aunt's brother. She visited here. She knew you. These other people, these friends—they all know you." She pressed her hands to her forehead. "This is crazy. And what about this man we've been calling Matthew Ettinger? Who is he? What lie is that?"

"That man," said Desiata, "is your uncle, Paul Farrow."

Claire slowly shook her head and sank back into the sofa. "I just can't believe it. How could you do this to me?"

"That's why I wanted to come," Desiata said. "I want to help you deal with all this, if I can."

"If you can? Now that no one is who I thought. Nothing is real. Nothing is true." She again shot to her feet, walked over to Farrow, and smacked him in the arm as hard as she could. "How could you?"

Desiata went to her. "Miss Fournaris … Claire … please, come sit."

She took a seat and put her head in her hands. "For the life of me, I don't know how all of this can be true. Coming here. The simplest of tasks—sign papers. That's all, just sign papers, visit my uncle, then go back home to my life, to my normal, ordinary life. But no. A car accident that was no accident. A driver who was not really a driver. Someone trying to throw me off the terrace. A dead nurse. Aunt Evelyn murdered." She looked up, her face flushed with fury and despair. "And all this time, I've been sheltered in this house. Everyone so nice. So helpful. So protective. Dinner parties and galas and a ride in the country and pumpkins, as if … as if …"

Desiata put his hand on Claire's shoulder. "I can only imagine what you are feeling right now."

"Betrayal," she said in a quiet voice. She looked up at Farrow. "That's what I'm feeling. You, of all people. And, who knows, maybe I'm about to find out that you're the one trying to do away with me. Why not? You've never known me. I became an intruder in your made-up life." She turned to Desiata. "I want to leave, Lieutenant. I want to go. Now. I don't want to hear anything. I don't want to know anything. I'm done. Done."

"Claire," Farrow said. "I've wanted to tell you. I tried to tell you. Please let me do it now."

"Let him explain," said Desiata.

"I trusted him," she said. "I began to … to like him … to feel as though I understood him. How could I possibly believe anything he says?"

"Because I'm here," said Desiata," and I'm asking, for now, just to trust me. Can you do that? Just for now?"

Without saying a word, she sat back, indignant, choosing not to look at either of them.

Desiata looked up at the man standing by the fireplace. "Why don't you start from the beginning?"

Chapter Twenty-Eight

"WE WERE COLLEAGUES, your uncle and I. Paul Farrow and I. Friends. Fellow architects. We designed and built things at the same firm. We collaborated. We worked well together, creating great buildings. Paul's work was his life. He was meticulous. He never married. Never made time to get that close to any woman, and that was too bad because he has always been a good man.

"My life was my family." He looked at Claire. "I'm the one who was married."

She blinked at him with a crimped brow as if attempting to bring him into focus. How was this possible? All these days in his house. So much time together—all of it fake.

"My wife's name was Robin. My young daughter's name was Bess. She loved horses. The year Bess turned seven, we went on vacation out west. There was a rodeo. Bess couldn't be happier. We had seats where she could see the entire arena. It was a beautiful place and a beautiful day. A warm day. They had a little concession stand, where I went to get cold drinks. I'm alive because I went to get cold drinks. I was not in my seat when the bleachers collapsed, killing my wife and daughter."

Claire sucked in her breath and looked at Desiata, the shock abating her anger.

"I didn't know how to cope with any of it. My world was gone. A double funeral. A requiem Mass. Two caskets at the altar. I had never seen a child's casket. Eternal grief." He paced slowly in front of the fireplace. "I couldn't work. I couldn't sleep or eat. The pain was unbearable. I wasn't prepared for it. I didn't know what to do with it.

"Your uncle knew how desperate I was. He was worried for me, more worried than I was. I wanted to die. He knew it. He didn't trust leaving me out of his sight. He insisted I come live with him, changed his work schedule, even stopped playing handball three days a week. He set up an office in his home, a beautiful home. He did everything to make it my home as well as his.

"I couldn't go back to my own house. I wasn't strong enough to face that. Paul was the one who sold it for me and moved all my things out. Everything. He removed special keepsakes that had belonged to my wife and my little girl and placed them in a box. I never went to that house again. And I still have never opened that box. I stayed in Paul Farrow's house. Evelyn came."

"She knew all this?" Claire said. "She knew what happened?"

"Your aunt was a kind and wonderful person. We became friends. She was the only person I allowed myself to get close to during that time." He took a deep breath. "The firm we worked for was very understanding. They gave me all the time I needed. Little by little, I began to open up until I needed to get back to work to keep my sanity. I found focus with a big project that your uncle chose for the two of us to work on together.

"But I had been so blinded by my own circumstances that I never noticed what was happening to him. He had become more driven than I realized. When I got up most mornings, it was clear that he had not been to bed. I'd find him at his drafting table by the window, sheets of blueprint paper scattered about the floor, cigarette butts overflowing the ashtray.

"The developer whose building we were working on was the biggest client our firm ever had. That *we'd* ever had. The building, an enormous elegant, apartment building, was slated for Madison Avenue, not far from Central Park, but the developer was located in Paris. We had not met. We had only spoken long-distance. When we were ready, Paul and I were to fly to Paris and present our design and blueprints. Our firm was counting on us. The pressure was enormous, and all this time, Paul's behavior was becoming more and more erratic."

Claire watched as this man, perhaps now more a stranger than ever, paced the floor. She had glimpsed his vulnerability once or twice before, this man of such strong presence now laying himself bare under the weight of his incredible secret. She had no idea what to make of it or even how to react.

"Whenever I tried talking to Paul about it, he flew off the handle, slamming doors and telling me I had no idea what I was talking about. Little did I know that on his trips to New

York City the year before, he had discovered the Opium market in Chinatown, and his addiction was now on full display."

"That's pretty sad to hear," said Desiata, who had sat as rapt as Claire.

"Evelyn never spoke a word about it," Claire said.

"No, but you recall telling me that she had come home more quiet than usual after her trips here."

"Yes," Claire said.

"Paul was becoming destructive. And not just self-destructive. He kept me locked out of his private office. I would hear things being thrown around. Once, when he was out, I managed to unlock the door and found our blueprints for the Paris client spread about, nearly ruined with burns and spills.

"I took them and salvaged what I could, completely redoing a number of them. At the same time, I contacted a small, private treatment facility for help. But Paul refused to go. He became furious and came at me with a poker from the fireplace. He had become a wild man. I had to knock him out to restrain him. Then I put him to bed, and locked him in his room.

"A few hours later, he was yelling and pounding on the door. I realized I would have to commit him somewhere. We were due to be in Paris the following week. I knew he wasn't fit to be part of it. The company's reputation, as well as ours, would suffer tremendously. They would no doubt lose their most valuable client. I couldn't let that happen. And you can be sure that Paul and I would both lose our jobs. More importantly, he needed serious help, more help than I could give him. I had no idea how to handle him.

"As I struggled to figure things out, fate stepped in. Sadly, Paul suffered a massive stroke. Now, I had a different problem—how to protect him. I owed him everything. I couldn't allow this once kind and brilliant architect to turn up at the hospital, a victim of opium and alcohol abuse, along with everything else. And that was the moment I hatched this whole crazy plan. I admitted him to the hospital, as Matthew Ettinger. Then, I called Evelyn. I had kept her informed all along about her brother. Still, the news was heartbreaking. She came immediately, and I told her of my plan. Several days later, I flew to Paris as Paul Farrow."

For a few moments in the study, there was only silence. Despite her feelings about being deceived, Claire couldn't overlook the magnitude of devotion for a self-destructive friend. She made eye contact with Desiata, who also seemed to have listened with a sympathetic ear.

"Just how did you manage this switch of identities?" Desiata asked. "Your company would know."

"Believe it or not, they didn't. I explained that I had come down with influenza, and that Paul would have to go to Paris alone. They had no idea that I was the one who was going to Paris in Paul's place. The client had never met me or Paul. So, it all worked out."

"Amazing," said Desiata.

"When I came back, I told them that Paul had had a great meeting with the client, but there was a family emergency involving Evelyn, his only family, and he'd had to leave immediately for Chicago. I told them I would finish the revisions. And I did."

Desiata scratched his chin. "But how was it possible for this ruse to continue?"

"Evelyn was in Chicago. I had her send a fake telegram from Paul to the company, telling them that he had to extend his stay there to care of his sister. A week after that, Evelyn sent another fake wire from Paul, telling them that he had no choice but to resign. I waited another week and resigned, as well. I told them I was going to take a break, then, likely start my own business. They expressed their disappointment, but wished me well.

"Paul was still in the hospital, heavily sedated. I knew what I had to do. In a nutshell, I sold Paul's house, added my own considerable funds to it, and bought this estate. A quiet place. Out of the way. No one here would know the difference."

"But if no one here knew the difference," said Desiata, why continue to be Paul Farrow?"

"Paul Farrow made some bad choices, but he was brilliant and a far more dynamic architect than I. He had helped so many other architects get their footing in the industry. I couldn't let Paul Farrow's name fade into oblivion when my world had become a place where I felt I was just marking time. So, I decided to do my best to continue his legacy. The Kaplan Manor in Chicago was the first."

"That was yours?" Claire said.

"As far as anyone knows, it was Paul Farrow's."

"But the money," Claire said. "You've been living on my uncle's money. Your great generosity. It was all my uncle's. I know he had a lot of money. Didn't it trouble you to use it for this … this lifestyle of yours? And what about David? Didn't he pick up on this? He was managing your accounts."

"No," Desiata broke in. "No, Claire. Your uncle's money was all gone. Let him explain. This is what caught my attention in the investigation." He made a casual gesture with his hand. "It always seems to be the money that gives everything away."

"I had set up two Paul Farrow accounts. David used one of them for everything we needed. I funded that account with a monthly deposit from the second Paul Farrow account. David saw this transfer every month. What he didn't … doesn't … know about is the third account I have. My personal account … Matthew Ettinger's … which has always funded the second Farrow account. David never knew that the money in Paul Farrow's account was coming from that third account in my real name."

"I don't know what to make of this," Claire said. "Your wife, your daughter. I'm so sorry for the heartbreak you must have suffered. Then my uncle. Tragedy upon tragedy. How many people would go through that much trouble to protect a friend?"

"I never saw your uncle as just a friend, Claire. You have to understand. He was my … in a way … my savior. He knew, as

I did, that I would have ended my life. It's only because of Paul Farrow that I'm even alive today."

Desiata sat back and shook his head. Claire put her face in her hands, then looked up. "And why call my uncle Teddy? What's the point of that?"

"You may not know that your uncle's middle name is Theodore. Some of his close friends called him Teddy, although I never did. Still, I didn't want him to be addressed by a name that wasn't his. What would that do to further his warped mental state? No, I had to give him something of his own. And, by the way, when he called out Vee, I knew exactly who he was referring to. He was attempting to say Evie. Evelyn. Apparently, your voice, Claire, resonated like Evelyn's. That's why I had to get him away. It disturbed him too much."

Claire got up and walked to the bookshelves. "I wish I knew what to say or how to feel. I don't seem able to navigate this … this maze of events and feelings and … and…"

"That's understandable, Miss Fournaris," said Desiata. "It's a lot to take in, even for me."

"There was one more thing," said Ettinger, "I hesitate to even say it, but I need you both to fully understand." He ran his fingers through his hair. "In those first few days when your uncle was hospitalized, I found thirty-five thousand dollars in his room. It was in a large brown envelope with our company's name on it. I knew immediately that he had embezzled it to fund his opium addiction. Now, my concerns had reached a whole new level. The company would eventually trace it to

Paul. I couldn't let that happen. Fortunately, right after they discovered it missing, I managed, by the grace of God, to put the envelope in a secure place at the office where it would be found. And, as puzzling as it was to everyone, they chalked it up to gross carelessness. Everyone got a memorandum about secure handling of company funds, and nothing more was made of it."

"Did you ever share any of this with anyone else?" said Desiata. "Anyone at all?"

"No. I never even told Evelyn about the embezzlement. I didn't want to add to her pain."

Claire, silent and intense, with more mixed feelings than she knew what to do with, said nothing. Finally, she turned to Desiata. "What will happen now, Lieutenant?"

"Well, he's not being charged with anything, if that's what you're thinking. Under the circumstances, I don't see that a crime has been committed." Desiata got to his feet and put his arm on Matthew Ettinger's shoulder. "Have a seat, Paul."

"Why are you still calling him Paul?" Claire blurted out.

"Yes," said Ettinger, "I'm confused."

"Look," said Desiata, "we still have a murder investigation going on. Matthew, you will continue to be Paul Farrow. Claire, you will continue to call him Paul or uncle. You must go on as if nothing has changed. No one must know a word of what has been spoken of in this room. No one. Because we now have to consider whether someone, somehow, also knows the truth and wants, for whatever reason, to keep it a secret.

And I believe he wants it to look like an accident to prevent an investigation that would reveal the truth, such as it is." Desiata stood looking at the fire, then turned. "Maybe your aunt was killed because she knew. Whether there is a connection or not, we still have a murderer on our hands, a murderer who's been a little too quiet now. This is a moment when murderers catch their victims off guard. So, be very careful."

Chapter
Twenty-Nine

Claire was relieved the next afternoon when David invited her for a leisurely ride, grateful for the diversion from the fresh layer of madness that would keep her captive not only to the estate but to the grand lie.

"Beautiful fall day, isn't it?" Wonderful David, so happily unaware. Over breakfast in the kitchen, he had jabbered on, teasing Farrow and Parmalee about this and that, flirting with Claire, praising Marjorie for her delicious waffles.

Claire had hurried through her meal, saying very little, eager to return to the long list of convention attendees, a tedious process that not only took her mind off everything else, but that she knew might yield some clue or connection to help Desiata. David's timing was perfect; she had been ready to take a break.

"How do you feel about seafood?" he said as they cruised the shoreline road. "Endio's is just up ahead on the right. The best in town."

They'd been out for more than an hour. "Sounds good," she said, noticing a black car that had been behind them nearly the entire drive as they leisurely skirted the Long Island Sound. She tried focusing on their surroundings to keep from becoming suspicious of everything. "Thank you for the outing, David. It's beautiful, and these homes are fabulous."

"Yes, and fabulously expensive. This whole area is what's called the Gold Coast. You can look across and see some of the different towns on Long Island's north shore."

Endio's Seafood Restaurant was a homey blend of red checkered tablecloths and dark wood with expansive windows that captured the autumn palette in a blazing landscape along the water's edge.

"You and Paul were tied up with the lieutenant for quite some time yesterday," David said, once they were seated. "Anything new? Paul's been a little off this morning."

"Nothing. Just more questions about the car accident and about how we found Marina." She wondered if David knew more than he was letting on. And it certainly had crossed her mind that if Paul Farrow wasn't really Paul Farrow, was David Preisler really David Preisler? Or Parmalee, or …

"Sorry you've had to go through all that, Claire. Maybe this little jaunt of ours will provide a happy shift."

She offered the biggest smile she could muster, wanting to believe this would be a happy excursion, until she noticed a familiar-looking black car in the parking lot.

"Haddock, sea scallops." David browsed the menu choices. "Although the Atlantic cod is always very good."

"David." Claire reached over, touching his hand. "There's a black car parked at the end of the restaurant. It's the same car that was behind us the whole time we were traveling along the water."

He peered out the window. "You mean that black Plymouth? That's such a popular car. There must be dozens of them on the road."

"One thing that the lieutenant said yesterday was that things have been a little quiet since Marina's death, and that can be a kind of … you know … kind of an easy time to catch a victim off guard."

David took Claire's hand. "I bet he also told you to be careful. Right? Well, here we are in a busy, friendly restaurant right out in the open in daylight. We can be out and about and still be careful, just like tomorrow night at Jakobiak's." He took a sip of coffee. "And by the way, that is going to be an experience. Trust me, Claire. The professor will not allow his dinner to be outdone by Marjorie Tarr's reputation. You can be sure of that. He'll pay a small fortune hiring the best caterer, then pretend it's, oh, just another routine meal in the life of Professor Arthur Jakobiak. He's quite the character."

"He seems like a nice man. And he's a good dancer; I know that."

"He is. And let me say again how good it was seeing you have a great time at the gala, even if …"

"Even if I was floating on champagne bubbles?"

They laughed.

"Say, I have an idea," he said, after the waitress had placed their steaming plates of blue crab and mussels before them on the table, along with the customary bibs. "Come dancing with me. Tonight."

"Dancing?" She looked down at herself. "But I'm not dressed for it."

"Your dress is perfect. In fact, everything about you is perfect."

She looked away, self-conscious.

"Listen, there's a nice little café in Milford with a great swing band. They play a lot of Benny Goodman. And you're dressed for it just the way you are."

"You'll have to call home, David, and let them know. Paul will be very upset if we're away so long without even saying where we are, especially after dark." She turned his wrist toward her to see his watch. "It'll be pretty late by the time we get home."

"I'll handle it; I promise."

For the next two hours, Claire enjoyed the food and the small talk, happy to be with someone who made it easy for her to put aside her anxiety, even for a while. As they gathered their jackets, she was relieved to see that the black Plymouth was gone. Twenty minutes later, they entered Noonan's Shore Club, which appeared almost as David had described—a nice place with great music, except not so little and a bit more upscale than she had expected. The place was packed.

After managing to get a small table near the back and place their drink order, they sat out enjoying a few swing tunes that kept the dance floor busy.

"This is fun," Claire said.

"I think it will be even more fun when we get out there for a slow dance."

"But first…"

"Yes, I know. First. I have to phone Paul." He looked about. "I'll go find a pay phone."

It all reminded her of the gala, except without the ballgowns and tuxedos—a noisy, joyful group having a good time, packed in nearly one upon the other. She couldn't help but smile. As she sat enjoying the music, waiting for David to return, she noticed a man at a table by himself in the corner. When he had caught her eye, he lifted his glass and nodded to her. She turned away, her thoughts falling quickly to suspicion. She looked about to see where David had gone, and when she turned back, the man was standing at her table. She jumped.

"Didn't mean to scare you," he said. He was a tall, thin man with dark blond hair and a grin too sly for Claire's taste or comfort.

"I'm sorry. I'm with someone," she said, looking away.

"No need to be sorry. I'm here to offer you a better choice."

She could smell the alcohol on his breath. "Please, excuse me," she said, her pulse quickening.

"Don't be that way," he said. He reached down and pushed David's drink aside, splashing some of it onto the table. "We can do better than this." He took her by the arm. "I would never leave you by yourself. We can have a very good time together. All you have to do is come with me."

His fingers were long and bony. She pulled away and got to her feet. Her distress, blotted out by the noise and bustle of the place, went unnoticed. He grabbed her arm again, coming closer, pushing her toward the entrance as servers carrying trays full of drinks maneuvered around the dance-floor crowd and the busy tables, oblivious.

"See, no one else is concerned. Why should you be?" The words seemed to fall in slimy curls from his wet lips. "Just come along and everything will be all right."

Claire managed to pull away, but he grabbed her again.

She kicked him in the shin.

"You'll come with me," he said in a loud whisper, his teeth clenched. The harder she resisted, the more menacing his glare.

As they passed one of the tables, Claire grabbed someone's drink and threw it in the man's face. The people at the table drew back, shouting their protest, while the assailant rubbed his eyes and went after Claire again, just as a familiar face appeared at Claire's side.

Edmund Parmalee leveled a single blow to the man's stomach that brought him nearly to his knees, then a backhand to his face that knocked him against the wall. Parmalee reached down and yanked the man's wallet from his back pocket. "I'll be taking this with me," he said, removing the driver's license. "We'll be interested in knowing just who you are and what you're up to. You will want to hope very hard that we find out that you are nothing more than a cheap masher." Parmalee threw the man's wallet at him and led Claire out the door as David came rushing through the dance-floor crowd.

"Oh, Edmund, Edmund, thank you! Thank God!" Claire was breathless as she clung to Parmalee's arm.

"You'll be fine now," he said. "And if you don't mind my saying, Miss Fournaris, throwing that drink in the man's face was a superb move, as was the shin kick." They broke into laughter as David caught up with them.

Then, after seeing David and Claire safely off in David's car, Parmalee got into his black Plymouth and followed them back to the house.

CHAPTER THIRTY

CLAIRE KNEW SHE couldn't go on ignoring Paul Farrow. Being together in the same house had been more awkward than ever after his shocking admission, but she would have to speak to him sooner or later, and she still didn't know what to say. Was she supposed to forgive him? And for what—deceiving her? Does that cancel out everything that he went through? Evelyn knew about it from the beginning, and it never diminished her opinion of this man. She went on with her life without any drama, although her brother's situation had to have broken her heart.

"Thank you for having Edmund follow us," she said to him over breakfast on Wednesday morning. "Things got a little out of hand last night."

"I heard."

"I'm sorry."

"I think those words should come from David instead of from you." He looked directly at her. "He seems to throw caution to the wind when it comes to being with you."

"Well, you would have to agree that it doesn't help the situation when I go along with it."

"That's understandable. It's probably because you care for him as much as he cares for you."

"I didn't say that."

"Do you have to? What's that old saying about actions speaking louder than words?"

"Paul … I …" But she trailed off, not knowing how to answer. David was a friend. She couldn't help that he liked her. She enjoyed his company, but …

"You don't have to explain yourself to me. I'm just your uncle, remember?"

The words cut like a razor. She took a deep breath and jumped to her feet, grateful that the others had already left the kitchen. "I came to this house with the best intentions. I didn't have to come, you know. My aunt's attorneys are in New York. But I came as family to meet this … this man that Evelyn loved so much. I expected that I would visit and likely never see you again. Believe me, I … I wish it were true. You deceived me. You manipulated me. For all I know, you'd be happy if the murderer succeeded in killing me—"

"Stop it!" The loudness of his voice shocked and silenced her. "Why don't you sit back down and listen?"

She remained standing, defiant.

He tossed his napkin onto the table and glared at her. "Better yet, come with me."

They left the kitchen, both in a huff of anger and frustration. She followed him to his study, where he locked the doors behind them. Then, he led her to his private study at the end of the room, the room she hadn't dared to fully enter.

He went behind his desk. "Come."

She stepped behind the desk near where he was standing, and there on a corner of his desk was a framed photo of her and Evelyn.

"Do you have any idea why this photo has been here for several years?"

"How could I?" She had softened her tone.

"Because as I grew in friendship with your wonderful aunt, I grew in some measure of … let's say … acquaintanceship … with you. I learned of your studies and your work. I heard the stories of your life, your activities, what you do, and who you are. That you love peonies and cocker spaniels."

Her heart started throbbing in her ears, her face radiating heat she was sure he could feel.

"I did not want you to come here. I did not want to get close to you. I knew I would have to tell you everything. Not since Robin had I imagined what strength of feelings I could have for someone else."

For a long moment, they studied each other in silence. How could she say a word now that he had touched upon her own secret—that she had felt a gnawing attraction for him nearly from those first days in the hospital, feelings she was ashamed to have and, now, much too embarrassed to admit. "I … I …" But she couldn't finish. She couldn't even start. She left his private office and crossed the study.

He stepped from behind his desk and stood in the doorway. "Sooner or later, Claire, you'll be free to return to Chicago, and we'll both get on with our lives, such as they are."

She stopped and turned to him. "Your words. Your feelings have … they have shocked me." She put her head down for a moment before looking up, her feet firmly planted, as someone fearful of yielding. "All I can bring myself to say … is that my own feelings … very possibly … might prove to be an even greater shock to both of us." She unlocked the doors and left.

He could not find her. Lucy hadn't seen her, neither had Parmalee. David had been looking for her himself. Farrow asked Marjorie. "Have you seen Claire?"

"Rollie told me she went shopping in town. She said she wanted something new to wear to the Jakobiak's dinner this evening."

"But all the cars are still in the garage," Farrow said. "How did Louis take her?"

"Oh, Louis didn't take her," Marjorie said. "Hannah Lillian picked her up."

Farrow swallowed hard and ran his hand through his hair, thinking of Claire off on her own. "Tell Rollie to have Louis bring the car around. I'll call Bob Lillian."

Marjorie touched his arm. "Is everything all right?"

"I have no idea," he said. "None at all."

Chapter Thirty-One

"I think Hannah said they were going to Molly's." Bob Lillian relayed the information in his typically jovial tone. "It's her favorite dress shop."

But they were not at Molly's and, according to the proprietor, they had not been there. After more than an hour driving through town, surveying dress shops, on the lookout for Hannah Lillian's burgundy colored Chrysler, they headed back to the estate, where Farrow immediately called Bob Lillian again. Hannah answered the phone.

"I … I just wanted to make sure," he said, "that Claire would be home in time to get ready for Arthur's dinner party tonight."

"I dropped her off half an hour ago, Paul. Isn't she there?"

He stumbled, embarrassed to admit he hadn't checked. "I just got in. I haven't seen her. I'm sorry for calling, Hannah."

"Is everything all right? You sound … I don't know … scared. I figured she must have told you."

Farrow felt his pulse quicken. "Told me what?"

"About this situation we had with another car."

"What kind of situation?"

"Well, right after we left Adrienne's—you know the place. The little dress shop on the shoreline near the ferry."

"I know the place."

"We started heading up Saugatuck River Road, and there was a car behind us. I didn't pay any attention to it, at first, but then, strangest thing, he got closer and closer, right on my bumper as if he was about to hit my car. I was going about forty, and I didn't want to speed up so close to town. But he stayed right behind me. And, I have to say, it got scary because when I went around that curve at the dockside, he started passing me too close near the water's edge there. He was clearly a very drunk driver. Luckily, a patrol car came up behind us and took off after him."

"Could you tell if it was a man or a woman driving, what kind of car it was?"

"The driver was hard to make out. Whoever it was wore a kind of wide-brimmed hat. And, honestly, all I know about the car is that it was a dark color. Black. Maybe dark brown. I never know one model from another. I'm so sorry, Paul, especially after what Claire went through with her car accident."

"I'm sure she'll be all right, Hannah. Thanks for letting me know."

"Then, we'll see you tonight. She's quite a girl that niece of yours."

Quite a girl, he thought, exasperated. Furious. He looked up and saw David and Claire walking toward him.

"Look who I found," David said.

"I'm sorry, Paul. I guess I was a little too impulsive. I shouldn't have gone out without letting you know."

"Did you have a good time?"

She hesitated. "Yes. I … bought a new dress. Hannah was so nice to take me."

"And she's such a good driver, isn't she, even with a car trying to push you off the road into the water?"

David looked at Claire. "Is this true?"

"I'm sorry. I know I acted impulsively by going. I was just feeling so …"

"I'll bet it never occurred to you," Farrow went on, "that you might be placing Hannah Lillian's life in jeopardy as well as your own. She doesn't know what's going on. She thinks it was a drunk. Maybe it was." He turned and headed toward the study. "Well, good. I'm sure Desiata's men could have fished you out of the water along with your new dress. With a little steam cleaning, the dress could have been all fixed up for you to be buried in. Eight o'clock. Let's all be ready."

David looked at Claire, shaking his head. "I can't imagine how you could do something so … irresponsible, to say nothing of dangerous. What were you thinking? Desiata said don't leave the estate alone. He meant don't leave the estate without one of us. He said trust no one. He meant no one. And here they go, driving all over town looking for you, for Hannah Lillian's car. And then you're nearly run off the road by who knows who. It's ridiculous! Why should we even bother to care anymore?"

"I am sorry, David. Truly."

David walked off without uttering a word as Claire remained there, feeling the weight of her own guilt. They were right, of course. There was no excuse for her lack of consideration. She headed to the kitchen.

Marjorie turned from the sink when she entered. "You look like you might be ready to enjoy a nice, hot cup of chamomile. Or would you prefer Earl Grey? The kettle is already on."

If only there was nothing more to trouble over than which tea to brew. If only she were free of killers and caution and the ever-growing shock of things. Something would have to change. If Desiata wasn't going to figure it all out, then she would somehow have to do it herself, and be done with it.

For lack of anything else to occupy her mind until it was time to dress for the dinner party, Claire took her cup of tea to the dining room and set her lists of convention guests in front of her on the table. Dozens and dozens of names, page upon page, and so far, she had come across only one name with the initials H. A.—Henrietta Alworthy from Bethel Heights, Arkansas. She kept looking.

As she turned through the pages, something happened, something that would change everything. Her eyes fell on those very first names that Lucy had checked. Lucy had not done what Claire had asked; she had misunderstood. And as Claire looked dismissively at Lucy's check marks, her back stiffened. Her heart began to race. Without either of them realizing it, Lucy had found something that stopped Claire cold. She gathered up the pages and hurried across the main floor to Paul Farrow's study just as Rollie Tarr came down the staircase.

"Is everything all right, Miss Fournaris? You look like a startled rabbit."

"I'm okay, Rollie. Honestly. I just have to see … my uncle." When she reached the double doors, she tapped lightly before entering, then a little harder when there was no response. She opened the doors and saw the light on in Farrow's private office at the far end of the room.

"I'm sorry to bother you, Paul, but I have to show you something." Amid the alluring sweetness of pipe tobacco, she could see he'd been working on his book. There were papers scattered across his desk,

"I'm a little busy right now."

"Please, Paul. This is not a time to hold on to hard feelings. Not only am I sorry for my part, but I am most in need of sharing this with you."

He set his pipe down and came from behind his desk. "Let's go into the study."

"I hadn't planned to disturb you, I promise, but you have to look at these pages." She took a deep breath. "Please."

She handed him the first pages, wondering if he would notice what she wanted him to see without her saying anything.

He glanced over the names, then gave her a questioning look.

"Look again," she said. "Look slowly. Pay careful attention to the ones marked with a red check."

Just as Claire had done, he looked more closely at each of the names with a red mark, the ones Lucy had mistakenly checked. A moment later, as if on cue, his eyes widened in complete surprise. "Is this telling me what I think it is? Is it even possible?"

"Remember what Desiata said—anything is possible."

"But this would be crazy," he said. "I don't know how it could be true."

"I don't know either, but we have to follow through with it, don't you think?"

` "Yes," he said, "of course." He paced in front of the fireplace.

"Shouldn't we call Desiata?" Claire asked.

He didn't answer at first. "Let's take a minute," he said, thoughtful, and led her to the sofa, where they sat in silence for a long moment, collecting their thoughts. "We've got to be very sure about this. It could be just a fluke. Or … it could be the most diabolical—"

"It would put a whole new slant on everything we've been thinking from the start," she said. "Everything."

"That it would."

There was a tap on the door and Tarr entered. "So sorry to bother, but I've got to leave for a while."

"Of course, Rollie. Is everything all right?"

"We're not sure. Bobby's gone. He left us a note."

"Oh, I'm so sorry," Claire said. "I hope he's okay."

Rollie Tarr handed the small folded paper to Farrow: "*I'm sorry, Aunt Marjorie and Uncle Rollie. But I must go away. I promise that I will call you. You have been so good to me, but I have to go."*

"I can call Lieutenant Desiata to see if he can help locate the boy," Farrow said.

"Trouble is," said Tarr, "he's not a boy anymore. And now that he's of age, he can go wherever he wants whenever he pleases."

"True, but it does sound as though he's troubled about something," said Farrow. "Do you have any idea what that might be?"

Claire looked at Farrow. "You recall I told you how nervous he seemed last week."

"Yes, and I spoke with him," Farrow said. "He said nothing was wrong but, clearly, there must be."

Claire went over to Rollie. "Let me ask you—did it seem to you that Bobby was more nervous than usual after I came here? It's okay. You won't hurt my feelings."

Rollie Tarr hesitated. "I can't explain the reason for it, Miss Fournaris, but I believe that is true."

"Let's do this," said Farrow. "Let's give it until tomorrow. He may return by then. If not, I'll call Desiata first thing and ask his help. Would that be okay with you and Marjorie?"

"Yes, thank you, sir."

"And, Rollie, please stop being so formal with me. Claire already knows that you and Marjorie are family around here."

When Tarr had left the room, Claire and Farrow looked at each other. "Well, isn't this turning into a day of days?" Farrow said.

Claire put her finger to her lip. "Do you suppose that there could be ..?"

"A connection between Bobby leaving and …" He picked up the list.

They sat back down. "Goodness," she said. "What's next?"

For a while, they sat in silence again, collecting their thoughts.

Then, he looked at her. A long, slow look. "Do you feel all right?"

"I'm fine. More or less. I might be getting used to the craziness. But now, with this, who knows? What made you ask that?"

"I think you look a bit pale."

"Listen," she said. "We have a lovely dinner party to go to in a little while. If you ask me, I think we should tuck this away in the back of our minds and just enjoy the evening."

He gave her another long look. "Okay. Maybe you're right," he said, clearly still absorbed in thoughts. "Besides, it's the first time you've been to the Jakobiak's, and the professor has a fabulous dinner planned. You can be sure of that. We are definitely going to have a good time." And with that, they sat for a while talking quietly, before Paul Farrow put his arm around Claire's shoulder and drew her to him."

"Edmund, did you see Bobby at all today?" Marjorie asked when Parmalee entered the kitchen.

"I can't say that I have. I've been out most of the day. I went to visit Matthew. Is anything wrong?"

"He's gone away. Here's the note he left us."

Parmalee took the note and read it. "I don't think there's anything to worry about, Marjorie. He's not a boy anymore. He probably just wants a chance to spread his wings a bit. Don't worry."

Marjorie continued putting a few things in the cupboard. "That's what Paul told Rollie. He said that if Bobby isn't back by tomorrow, he would call that lieutenant and ask for help."

"Desiata?" Parmalee said. "That's interesting. Well, we'll just hope for the best. I'm sure the boy will be okay."

She went to the table and took a seat next to Parmalee. "You know, Edmund, the boy has been more nervous than usual since Miss Fournaris arrived."

"I believe I've noticed that too," said Parmalee.

"Can I fix you some supper?" she asked, rising from the table.

"Thank you, no. I had a bite to eat while I was in town earlier today."

There were many thoughts scrambling playfully through the killer's mind—how to get her alone, catch her unaware, if only for the briefest of moments. That's all it would take. The briefest of moments when she might have set caution aside, let down her guard. It was long past time for Claire Fournaris to meet her fate.

Chapter
Thirty-Two

The laughter was contagious. Over a fabulous dinner of Beluga caviar, little neck clams, oyster crabs, and consommé, followed by breast of duck, lyonnaise potatoes, artichoke hollandaise, and candied squash, Claire and Farrow joined in with the others around Professor Arthur Jakobiak's joyful grand dining table. Once again, it was Bud Thomas regaling them with stories, this time about his first days as a veterinarian in lower Manhattan during the 1920s, treating everything from chickens that wouldn't lay eggs to sway-backed peddler-wagon horses that had been fed too much ice cream by the local children.

Dessert was a spectacular assortment of French pastries along with a platter of camembert and edam cheeses, red seedless grapes, and Turkish coffee accompanied by Armagnac French brandy, and pineapple water ice. Claire glanced at Paul Farrow. How strange for the two of them to be so caught up in the laughter, having only two hours earlier come upon what might be the shocking clue that identified a cunning murderer in their midst.

"Well, it is wonderful," said the Professor, "for Patrice and I to have you all around our table once again. And," he looked at Claire, "a new member in our happy little group. Beautiful Claire."

She dropped her eyes, embarrassed, as the others acknowledged her by raising their wine glasses.

"Here, here," said Bob Lillian.

"We couldn't have imagined anyone as sweet and engaging," said Miriam Gomshay, "to join all the wonderful friends here."

"Thank you so much. Every one of you," Claire blushed. If they only knew what had really been going on these past few weeks. "It has been such a pleasure to meet you, to get to know you, and enjoy your company."

Professor Jakobiak clinked his glass to hers. "Well, all I can say is thank God you made it out of that frigid water. Dead of night. Freezing cold. I'm not sure if any of us can quite imagine what went through your mind."

Bob Lillian turned to his wife. "Looks like you've got some swimming competition, Hannah."

"That's true," said Miriam Gomshay. "Did you know, Claire, that our delightful friend here was not only an Olympic tennis star, but quite a swimmer as well? Stockholm in 1912, and then … what was it? Oh, yes, Antwerp in 1920."

"Well, I only coached at Antwerp," said Hannah. "Age shows up quickly when you're an athlete."

Claire looked at this woman whom she'd gone out with for a shopping day, without having any idea of her amazing accomplishment. "That's remarkable, Hannah. How long did you have to train for that?"

"Frankly, all the time. Just train and train and train. But when you're young, you can do it."

Bob put his arm on his wife's shoulder. "True, but you know you could still compete with the best of them. They even invited her to coach the US team in Los Angeles in 1932."

"Oh, my goodness," Hannah laughed. "By then I was ready to just stay home and crochet."

"So, you see, Claire," said Patrice, who had remained a bit more reserved than was typical of her, "not only are you lovely, sweet, and kind, but you are also quite the survivor—strong and resilient. Wouldn't you agree, David?"

"You don't have to convince me." He laughed, as Farrow shifted in his seat, "All things considered, it's been the best couple of weeks I've had in a long time."

Lucy Conant chimed in. "It's true. David has somehow discovered patience for the first time in his life." The comment brought more laughter.

It was a lovely, elegant home, and yet not quite as full of the welcoming comforts of Paul Farrow's estate. It made her realize all the more how fond she was of the place and the people so connected to it.

"But, Lucy," Patrice said, "I imagine that since Claire's business is now resolved, she'll be leaving us soon, and David will be back to his old impatient ways."

"Maybe not," said Paul Farrow, taking everyone at the table by surprise, especially Claire and David. He turned to look directly at Claire. "My niece says she likes it here. Isn't that right?"

"Yes … that's right. I do."

Hannah Lillian clasped her hands together. "Well, then, that's wonderful news."

"It sure is," said Bud Thomas. "That means there might be more gala tangoes. Am I right, Claire Fournaris?"

She smiled. "I suppose you are."

"Say, speaking of galas," said Lyle Gomshay, "let's not forget to raise a glass to our man of the hour, our very competent host, to say the least, Professor Arthur Jakobiak. My compliments on such a wonderful dinner."

The evening moved along with toasts and laughter and good stories and well wishes for all, which Claire saw as nothing less than a refreshing trickle of water in the vast desert of angst and fearfulness. She felt grateful, and without thinking, she touched her foot to Paul Farrow's, then quickly pulled it away. A moment later, he touched his foot to hers, and left it there.

"I agree with Dr. Gomshay. This dinner has been very, very nice, Professor," she said. "I do believe even Marjorie would say as much. Thank you."

The group had finished their after-dinner drinks and began bringing the evening to a close. Jakobiak's butler, Edward, helped with coats before people ventured into the deep chill of the October night.

As Farrow and Claire moved toward the door, she stumbled. Farrow quickly reached for her, as did David.

"Oh, dear," said Hannah Lillian, "are you okay?"

"I'm fine," Claire said, "Can't imagine what happened. No champagne this time." She stumbled again.

"Please," said Miriam Gomshay, "come sit for a minute."

"No need, really," said Claire. "I'm … I'm …"

Farrow caught her as she nearly slipped to the floor. "Miriam is right. Come sit." "I don't know what's … what's going on," Claire said. "Just a little woozy."

"You can take her to my room," Patrice said.

Dr. Gomshay hurried to Claire's side with the brown leather medical bag he had with him at all times and began checking her vitals. "Your blood pressure is very low. Let's get her home, Paul. I'll go with you. I can give her something."

David stepped forward. "Shouldn't we take her to the hospital?"

"No need for that at the moment," said Gomshay. "It might be something very simple. We'll know in a little while."

Chapter Thirty-Three

For the next few days, the Farrow estate was busy with calls and visits, everyone concerned about Claire's dire condition.

"I just can't believe it," said Lucy. "She always seemed so healthy even after what she'd gone through with the car accident."

"I had no idea, either," said Paul Farrow. "She never said anything about a heart condition. Not a word. Neither had Evelyn."

Lyle Gomshay had let everyone know that following the hospital tests, he had prescribed a few medications as well as strict bed rest, hopeful that surgery would only be a last resort, and even then, there were no guarantees. He made it clear that she must remain calm and that the slightest excitement could have the most severe consequences.

A large fruit basket had arrived from the Lillians along with a dozen roses from the professor and another dozen from Bud Thomas.

Patrice Jakobiak came by to speak with Claire. She sat on the edge of the bed and put her hand on Claire's. "I wanted to confess how jealous I have been, and I'm sorry. It's just that every time I saw you and Paul together, it was clear that you have the kind of closeness that he and I have never had. And I realize we never will."

Claire gave a weak but appreciative smile. "Thank you, Patrice."

David dug his hands in his pockets and paced. "I'm worried, Paul. This sounds serious."

"I'm afraid it is. And there doesn't seem to be much we can do, except wait."

They were in the study along with the Professor, who wondered why Gomshay had not put her in the hospital.

"Because there's nothing they can do, Arthur. There's nothing any of us can do."

"She's that weak?" said Jakobiak.

Farrow set another log on the fire. "She's that weak, and Lyle says that the slightest excitement could … could …"

Jakobiak got up and pressed Farrow's shoulder. "Let's not think the worst, Paul. Let's pray that all will be well."

Farrow turned to David. "Are you staying?"

"I will, yes. I just have to go home and get some things."

"That's good. I can use the company."

"Why?" Jakobiak asked. "Where is everyone?"

"Marjorie's sister needed help with something. So, they're over in Litchfield. Edmund went with Louis to … who knows where … to pick up some part for one of the cars. They'll be a while."

"Well, then," said Jakobiak, "looks like you're stuck with me and a little game of chess. What do you say?"

"I say that's the best offer I've had all day, Arthur. Thanks."

After David left, the professor set up the chess board as Farrow excused himself to go up and check on Claire.

"How is she?" Jakobiak asked when Farrow returned.

"Resting comfortably." He ran his hand across his chin. "But I'm very worried, Arthur. The slightest … anything … could be … God help me, I hate to say the word. Fatal." He poured a small sherry for Jakobiak and himself, and began to play. "You'll beat me for sure tonight, Arthur. You can see how distracted I am."

"Ha. No excuses, my friend."

When the phone rang, Farrow left the table to answer it, and for a long moment said nothing. "It's okay, Rollie. Just stay put, and make sure that you and Marjorie are in a safe place." Farrow hung up the phone and rubbed his hands together nervously. "Arthur, I have a very special favor to ask."

"Ask away, Paul. What's going on?"

"Something happened to Rollie's car. They're stuck about fifteen minutes from here. I've got to go get them. Do you think Patrice can come and stay while I'm gone?"

"Patrice? Listen, my good man. I raised that girl. I think I'm still capable of looking after one more." He caught Farrow's eye. "Seriously, Paul. Everything will be okay. I know how to reach

Lyle if anything happens, but it shouldn't. Claire is resting, and you won't be long."

"Okay, then," Farrow said. "But do not, under any circumstances, answer the door for anyone. No one. Don't let anyone in. No matter what."

"Say, what's going on?"

"I really can't explain right now, but promise me. No one. The others can all let themselves in when they get here."

"Is there something you're keeping from me?"

"I'll explain later. Can you do this for me?"

"Of course." Jakobiak walked Farrow to the door and locked it behind him. Then, he turned and looked about at the great empty space. "Quiet as a tomb," he said to himself.

Chapter
Thirty-Four

Not long after Farrow left, a shadowy figure moved in the darkness of Claire's bedroom. *That poor fool of a professor could not possibly know a thing about what will happen here. How could he, beautiful Claire? There will be no evidence, just a quiet passing into eternity, and all will be right again.*

The figure drew nearer and nearer to Claire until close enough to whisper. "Claire. Claire, my dear, lovely woman, can you hear me? Open your eyes. I want you to see my face with a fear greater than your weak little heart can tolerate."

Claire opened her eyes and gasped at the maniacal face beaming evil.

"Too weak to scream, aren't you, my dear?

Her eyes widened, and she gasped again, clutching her chest, clutching it tighter and tighter with barely a whimper before her eyes closed, and her head rolled softly to the side.

With a throaty chuckle, the shadowy figure turned in triumph, then stopped short as the lights went on and Lieutenant Desiata stood in the doorway of the room. The terrace doors opened, and two police officers stepped in, guns drawn, Paul Farrow behind them.

Claire sat up in bed, and Farrow went to her as Professor Arthur Jakobiak stood frozen in the moment.

"You all tricked me." He raised an eyebrow. "Very nicely done."

"You did most of the tricking, Arthur," said Farrow. "That first day when Claire arrived at the house, and you took sick. You weren't sick. You fled because you were afraid Claire might be able to identify you. After that, you got conveniently sick so you could commit murder. That's what you did the night you pretended you were unable to finish our chess game, and I left. But so did you. Once you found out that Claire was going to see Marina Foge, you went and killed her."

"You even deceived them," said Desiata, "by saying you came across a man in the woods."

"Arthur, how could you?" Farrow asked. "You killed Evelyn. You killed the Village Taxi driver and Marina Foge. Claire would have been next. What happened to you? You were one of my dearest friends."

"It was for that exact reason. I've known all along who you really are," said Jakobiak. "Funny thing about anthropologists— we tend to notice things others don't. Ears, for example. Evelyn and that poor man you've been calling Matthew—they have the same ears. Did you ever notice? Yours are quite different."

"But what difference on earth would any of this make?"

"When people know things, sooner or later those things come out. Same with our lovely Claire." Jakobiak turned to her. "I'm so sorry, my dear. I knew that once you arrived, you would somehow find out that he is not your uncle, and that would throw my entire life into disarray. The same reason I had to kill Evelyn to protect our great little secret. I came back from Tel Aviv two days early, but I didn't come here. I went to Cincinnati to … well, you know. That's where Evelyn was. I had to do it. If it got out about you, Farrow, or should I say, Ettinger, there would be questions about your motive. Your reputation might be greatly damaged. Then, of course, mine would be as well. My foundation. My entire lifestyle. Complete disarray. You can understand why I couldn't allow that, I'm sure."

"And Marina Foge?" said Desiata.

"She had the button. The one I lost the night I tried to kill Claire in the hospital. I'm curious, my friend," said Jakobiak. "What happened to the suspect with the initials H.A.?"

"That was a mistake," Claire explained. "The medic who treated Marina told us that she uttered the initials H.A. That sent us looking in the wrong direction until I happened to notice the names that Lucy Conant checked off on the list of people who had attended the convention Evelyn went to. Where you murdered her. A couple of those names were Amelia Johnson and Anthony Jorgensen. Lucy had misunderstood me, but she got it right. Marina wasn't saying H.A. She was saying A.J. They sound so nearly the same, don't they, and that's why Marina looked so frantic just before she took her last breath—she saw that we had gotten it wrong. A.J.—the initials on that button she found. A.J. for Arthur Jakobiak."

"You confirmed our suspicions the other night at your dinner party, Arthur," said Farrow, "when you commented on Claire having made it out of the water the night of the accident. David and Louis did not find Claire on the bank. You had pulled her back into the water. So, only the killer would know that she had made it out of the water."

Desiata stepped closer to Jakobiak, "And by the way, we picked up Bobby Tarr trying to hop a freight train out of Hartford. He told us everything about how you coerced him into giving you Claire's arrival information by threatening to tell the police he had stolen from you. He'd had no idea what you were planning. He was terrified of going back to jail. He's not terrified anymore."

"You did horrible things to innocent people," said Claire, "for which I now pray you pay dearly."

Desiata motioned to the officer. "Get him out of here."

The weeks that followed were difficult. Patrice Jakobiak, unable to process her father's crimes or accept the kindness of friends, booked passage on the Queen Mary headed for France. Farrow's little circle of close friends, shocked by his true identity but still grateful for his friendship, accepted him now as Matthew Ettinger. The one who had the hardest time was David, who now clearly saw the handwriting on the wall regarding Ettinger's relationship with Claire, and although he would remain a close friend to both, left for another opportunity in New York.

Claire's uncle, Paul Farrow, died quietly in his sleep shortly before the new year and was laid to rest in Chicago with his sister Evelyn. Edmund Parmalee was urged to stay on but decided to pursue a long-dreamed-of career as a private investigator. Marjorie and Rollie Tarr remained and enjoyed helping Matthew and Claire arrange a fabulous wedding celebration at the estate for Louis and Lucy Joel. And two months later, just as spring was settling in, the estate hosted a second wedding.

THE END

ABOUT THE AUTHOR

 Mary Flynn is an award-winning author of fiction and poetry, as well as a celebrated speaker. A highly diverse writer, Mary has medaled in nearly all of her genres. Her powerful debut novel, "Margaret Ferry," won a gold medal in fiction, a silver medal in religion, and a silver medal in Christian writing. Her Disney leadership book is also a silver medal winner, while her novella for middle-grade readers took gold at The Royal Palm Literary Awards. And "No Small Wonder" continues to rate five-star ratings.

A former full-time staff writer for Hallmark Cards, Mary's observational humor has appeared in the *Sunday New York Times, Newsday* and other dailies and magazines. One of her award-winning short stories appears in the esteemed *The Saturday Evening Post's Anthology of Great Fiction*. She was a winner in the *Writer's Digest* poetry competition. She is also a writing coach, conducting writer's studios across Central Florida.

During her nearly fifteen years as an international conference speaker for Disney Institute, the second most recognized training brand in the world, Mary appeared before almost three-quarters-of-a-million people, often sharing a conference platform with names such as Malcolm Gladwell and Tony Robbins. She has been an on-air radio host for Salem Media, and loves entertaining audiences with her fun and informative "Confessions of a Hallmark Greeting Card Writer."

Mary's books are available online and through bookstores, as well as through her website.

Be sure to visit Mary at »
www.MaryFlynnWrites.com